MILO'S GIFT

By

Tom Nolan

Published by

MILLROCK

WRITERS

New Paltz, New York, U.S.A.
www.millrockwriters.com

ISBN-13 978-0-9792293-6-7
ISBN-10 0-9792293-6-7

Edited by Wanda Haskel
Cover Designed by Stacy Greenspan

For more information about books published by us and links to our authors visit -

www.millrockwriters.com.

Also by Tom Nolan –

Wishbone Creek and Other Stories - 2013

Second Cutting – 2014

For additional information and some links to
more goodies please visit -

www.gunkswriter.com.

Acknowledgements

To the fall and winter weeks spent writing at 'The Dog' and the folks there who give me the honest feedback I need, thanks.

To Carol – Always

Part I
The Dead Man

Milo's Gift

Chapter 1

The boy ran through the old forest, agile as a squirrel in the treetops, leaping over downed logs without breaking stride, leathery bare feet impervious to the occasional stone in his path.

"Maw! They's a dead man in Skunk Holler!" He skidded to a halt in front of the small cabin, scattering four scrawny hens near the step. "Maw!"

A woman emerged around the near side. "Hush boy, I'm not deaf." She approached him, her bare feet raising small dust clouds, her toed-in stride giving a sensuous sway to her thin hips, her threadbare shift dress damp with sweat. "Slow down and tell."

The boy took two gasping breaths and told his story. When he'd finished she asked, "Was there blood? Did you see any marks on him?"

"Didn't git that close, but he wadn't movin' a lick."

"Take me there."

On the trip back to Skunk Hollow, the boy dashed ahead like an eager puppy returning only to hurry her along. She knew they were near when he didn't return. Rounding a copse of hemlocks, she saw him perched atop an ancient white oak stump. He waved her forward without turning, pointing into the gully, his body rigid as a bird dog. She joined him on the stump, eyes following his arm and hand to the end of the steady finger.

The supine man had his arms spread wide as if being measured for a cross. The boy reached for her hand, held it. He glanced at her for only an instant, reluctant to take his eyes from his find. "He's dead, fer sure." Receiving no answer he turned the statement into a question. "Ain't he?"

"Let's go see," she answered. She scanned the area for a way down to the stream below. Spotting a game trail, she walked toward it, her mind pouring through the medical archive that was her Air Force nurse's brain so long ago. The boy followed. They slipped and slid down the narrow trail into the hollow and slogged through the ankle-deep chill of the mountain stream, finally reaching the inert form. She knelt beside him, felt the carotid artery and found a pulse, faint but steady.

The woman squeezed the boy's hand. "Is the stone boat empty?"

"Yeah?"

"Run back and harness Rosie to it. Bring her around by the old coal road over to there." She pointed to a low spot on the ridge just above. "Bring that stout rope hanging in the shed, hurry." She nudged the boy. "No, he isn't dead." She watched him scramble up the slope and disappear into the underbrush.

She inventoried the man from head to toe looking for signs of injury. Nothing. She stood frowning then shrugged. Recognizing that if he had a spinal injury he'd die before they traveled the thirty-five miles to get medical help, she turned him over gently as she could. Seeing no trauma aside from some minor scrapes that she attributed to his journey down the slope, she checked for broken bones again just for thoroughness, then sat back on her haunches.

His clothes were town, low-cut leather-soled shoes, dark brown cuffed trousers, and a green polo shirt. She checked his head again looking for any sign of trauma that would account for his condition but still found nothing. She stared at his still form, trying to come up with a set of circumstances that would have put him on her mountain.

4

The sound of the boy urging Rosie along the low ridge snapped her to attention. She rose and waved, pointing to the spot where she wanted him to stop. When he'd reined the mule in, she hollered, "Tie an end of that rope to Rosie's harness and toss the other to me." The boy looped a bowline into a hitch ring and flung the coil in a long arc. She watched it straighten like a striking adder as it fell toward her.

She grabbed the rope, puzzling a bit while she looked at the man. Finally she wrestled him to a sitting position, looped it under his arms then pinned his arms to his sides with another loop and tied it off with a double half hitch. Satisfied, she turned toward the boy.

"Walk Rosie away from the hill, slow now, and listen for me in case I want you to stop."

The boy clucked, tapping the reins on the mule's rump; she stepped out pulling the line taut. The limp form shifted in its tether, lined up along the direction of the rope then began sliding up the slope. The woman duck-walked beside him to be close enough to hold his head away from any rocks in their path. When they'd reached level land at the top, she ordered, "Stop. Back Rosie up." While she busied herself untying the man, the boy brought Rosie and the empty stone boat up beside them. He helped her lift the man onto the platform, though she didn't need the help, and tie him down.

The boy guided Rosie along the road, turning the mule at the entry to the clearing where their cabin and four other buildings stood. Watching the limp form flop around on the rough ride home made her wonder whether she'd imagined that faint pulse.

"Take him to the tool shed," she said, veering off toward the cabin, "I'll be right back." Inside, she went immediately to the footlocker at the foot of her bed, flung it open, extracted two olive-drab wool blankets, and shook out the cedar chips.

In the tool shed the woman and boy stuffed straw into a large wooden feed trough. She padded it further with one of the blankets then went outside to where the boy stood staring at the man's body.

"You sure he ain't dead?"

"I'm sure." She knelt beside the man and sat him up, holding him with her left hand while she lifted his shirt. "Help me take this off." They wrestled off his polo shirt and undershirt. Small tufts of dark hair outlined the nipples on the man's thin bare chest. The woman moved to his feet and unlaced his shoes, removing them and his argyle socks, revealing similar tufts of hair on each of his long toes. She unbuckled his belt. "Help me with his pants," she said, unzipping the fly and opening the waistband. She felt each of his pockets as she wrestled the trousers off his hips, finding nothing in any of them.

"He gonna be nekkid?"

She smiled. "His clothes are damp from the gully; he'll be more comfortable without them." They tugged the trousers off, leaving the man in his dingy white boxer shorts. "We'll dry them in the sun. Grab his legs."

They carried the man into the tool shed and settled him onto the makeshift pallet. She covered him with the other blanket, felt his neck again, found the faint pulse and stepped back shaking her head.

"He daid?"

"I already told you, no. Now scoot!" she said, shooing him out of the shed ahead of her.

While the boy went about his chores, the woman sat on the edge of the porch, feet swinging above the ground. She chewed her lower lip, then nodded and hopped down, glancing toward the small pasture where the boy was busy releasing Rosie from her harness. She entered the shed, strode over to the man and sat him up. He flopped forward till his head rested on his knees. Several small scars on the right side of his back led her to examine his head again. Pouring through the thick shock of brown hair, she located one tiny scar at the base of his skull. "Bet it's still in there," she said, setting him down gently.

That evening, after checking the comatose man for any change and finding none, she sat at the rough-hewn kitchen table watching the boy wolf down his meal, puzzling about what to do next. The man needed fluids if he was to survive but without an IV how could she manage it? A feeding tube maybe? She shook her head. What did they have that would do? She thought about sending the boy to Jethro's and having the old man go to Arkville to bring back help, but whoever came back with him would start asking questions. No, they'd have to deal with this on their own.

"Whut we gonna do with the man, Maw?" The boy said, rising to clear the table.

She shook her head. "I don't know yet."

"Whut's wrong with him?"

"He has shrapnel ..." seeing the question develop in the boy's eyes she added, "little pieces of metal – in his head, and it's pressing on a part of his brain that made him go into a coma, a really deep sleep."

"When he gonna wake up?"

"I don't know," she answered. "Now, get your arithmetic book." The boy trudged over to the ladder that led to his tiny loft. He climbed up and disappeared for a moment, returning with a battered textbook. He drew his chair around the table to sit beside her.

They worked on multiplication and division for the next hour, the boy's attention frequently wandering, and the woman varying the lesson to bring him back, an intellectual dance they'd been doing since she'd started tutoring him seven years before.

By the end of the hour they were both exhausted. She kept reminding herself that all she wanted was for him to gain enough schooling to function in a world he may never encounter. He was a child of the earth, knowing more about the animals and plants of the hill country at fifteen than most people would ever learn. He taught her secrets of the life around them that had helped them survive, things no book could teach, things learned from keen observation and an animal instinct unheard of in most humans. She only worried about how the rest of humanity would react to him and he to them. She needed to prepare him for the possibility.

After the boy climbed the ladder to his loft and she could hear his regular breathing, the woman picked up the oil lantern and walked into the dark night. She shivered as the cool mountain breeze ruffled her dress. At the tool shed she listened for movement before she opened the door. Inside, with only the orange glow of the lantern, she could see no rise and fall of the wool blanket that would indicate breathing. She hung the light on a hand-forged hook in the beam just above her head, squatted on her haunches beside the pallet and pressed two fingers on the carotid artery. The faint steady pulse greeted her as before.

"What am I going to do with you?" she mumbled, standing hands on hips, gnawing on her lower lip. As she turned to leave, a choking cough from the pallet froze her for an instant. Spinning on her heel, she reached the man's side in two steps. She knelt and hauled him to a sitting position, holding him there while he caught his breath.

When his cough subsided and his breathing quieted, he turned his face toward her.

"Where am I?"

"Don't worry about that just now." She checked his pulse, finding it strong, if a little rapid. "My boy found you in the woods. He thought you were dead."

The man shook his head, trying to clear it. Shivering, he looked down at his bare torso. "Where are my clothes?"

She retrieved them from the bench where the boy had dropped them before dinner and tossed them onto the blanket at his feet. He started to rise then stopped, looking at her.

The woman smiled. "You don't have anything I haven't already seen. Put them on." He reached for the trousers, felt the pockets. "They were empty when I took your pants off." When he frowned, she added, "You think I'd haul you out of the woods to rob you? Put your damn clothes on and let's get you some food."

After he dressed, she led him up to the cabin. Motioning to one of the kitchen chairs she picked up her plate from the drainboard, opened the breadbox and broke off a large chunk from the remaining half of yesterday's sourdough loaf. Adding two strips of venison jerky from the cupboard, she set the food in front of him then pumped a cup of water from the stone sink and placed it next to the plate. She sat across the table while he ate, watching his hands and head for any twitches that might signal another seizure.

The man glanced up from his meal, meeting her gaze. "Why are you staring at me?"

"Observing," she answered. "Just keeping an eye out for signs you might pass out again." He frowned and returned to the bread and jerky.

9

Taking a long drink from the cup, the man sat back in the chair. "Thanks. That was good."

She grinned. "You must have been pretty hungry then."

"My name's Robert."

"Jenny." She nodded in the direction of the loft. "The boy's name is Milo. How did you end up in Skunk Hollow?"

"Is that where I am?" He shook his head. Glancing at his wrist, he slapped the table with the flat of both hands, startling the woman for an instant. "Jesus, my watch, too!" He glanced over his shoulder in the direction of the loft then lowered his voice. "Sorry, I hope I didn't wake him."

"You didn't," she said. "He's been awake since you walked through the door." She looked past him. "Milo, it's okay. Go to sleep now." Rustling noises came from the loft then silence.

"I thought we were pretty quiet coming in. How did we wake him?"

"The noise didn't wake him. It was your scent." Seeing his question forming in his eyes, Jenny intercepted it. "He has a nose like a bloodhound." she stared at him, frowning.

"What?"

"Have you blacked out like that before?"

"Yeah," he said. "Last time was ... maybe seven years ago. Yeah. Nineteen eighty-five. I woke up in a hospital in Nashville." He leaned back in the chair. "They said I'd been there eight days." He closed his eyes. "Somebody found me lying in the road or something."

"Before that?"

10

"A couple of times since …" he straightened in the chair. "Why are you asking?"

"I'm just wondering whether I've got to worry about you passing out again."

Robert nodded. "Hasn't happened that way before." He leaned forward. "By the way, where am I? I mean, where's Skunk Hollow?"

"Middle of nowhere. About thirty-five miles from Arkville as the crow flies, more like fifty if it has to use the roads." Jenny rose. "You want more bread or jerky?" He shook his head. She leaned across the table to pick up the plate, noticing that Robert's eyes focused briefly on the open neck of her dress. She resisted the urge to grasp the fabric with her free hand, straightened, and walked toward the sink. Imagining his eyes on her as she moved, Jenny felt her face flush. "Morning comes early around here. You'd best be getting some rest," she said without turning. "We'll try to improve your accommodations tomorrow." At the sound of the chair scraping along the wood floor Jenny held her breath, expelling it only when she heard the door open and close.

She filled the cast iron kettle, put it on the stove and poked the waning fire to life. Adding a small maple split from the wood box, she walked to the space below Milo's loft that served as her bedroom and sat on the edge of the small bed. She smoothed the threadbare dress down over her knees with calloused hands then stood and slipped it over her head. Naked in the glow of the single candle, Jenny padded over to the sink and hauled the small washbasin off the shelf above it. She retrieved the kettle and poured the warm water into the basin, tested it with her free hand and put the kettle on the table. Grabbing soap and a cloth from the sink she washed quickly, emptied the basin and refilled it with fresh water, rinsed the soap off and dried herself on a towel that had been warming near the stove. She padded back to the bed, climbed under the blanket and closed her eyes.

Chapter 2

The dawn had barely begun when she heard Milo climb down the ladder and tiptoe toward the door.

"Look around by the hollow and see if you can figure out how Robert got there." The boy nodded on his way out.

Jenny rose and slipped her dress on. She brushed her hair back with her fingers, retrieved the kettle from the table and refilled it at the sink then set it on the stove. She teased the fire to life, added another maple split and watched until it caught. Turning away from the stove, she looked through the window at the door of the tool shed in the beam of the morning sun. "What am I going to do with you?" She recalled reading something Lee Iacocca once wrote about not making a decision until you have to. "Good advice, Lee," she said, punctuating the statement with a single nod before grabbing two cups from the shelf and placing them on the table. Smiling and shaking her head she went back for a third.

By the time Milo returned, Jenny had sourdough biscuits in the oven and was whipping a half dozen eggs while the cast-iron skillet warmed.

"Find anything?"

"Wadn't no car track on the coal road since last rain," Milo reported. "Somebody walked in carryin' him, from the big road looks like. That's a fur piece." He went to the sink and gave his hands a cursory rinse. "Had to be someone big as Jethro, mebbe bigger." He wiped his hands on his shirt.

"Tell him breakfast will be ready shortly," she said, nodding toward the tool shed. Milo scooted out the door.

When he returned a few minutes later, Robert on his heels, Jenny had biscuits on the table. She scooped eggs from the skillet onto three plates.

"Good morning, Jenny."

"Morning." She nodded toward Milo, who had plopped into his customary seat at the table. "Milo says somebody carried you from the main road." She pointed to the far corner of the room with the wooden spoon in her hand. "Pull that chair up to the table and sit."

"He told me," Robert said, retrieving the chair. He turned to look at the boy. "Milo, how do you know?"

"Wadn't no tire tracks on the coal road. I ranged some 'n found track leadin' back that way. Followed it a bit 'n saw where it was comin' from."

"But how do you know it wasn't me?"

"You ain't big enough. Tracks are deep, feet are big as Jethro's."

"That's a neighbor a mile or so down the hill," Jenny explained.

Milo frowned at the interruption then continued. "Tracks stop on the ridge above Skunk Holler 'n they's sign sayin' he dropped you 'n let you roll."

Robert nodded.

"Coffee?" Jenny asked, carrying the dark blue enameled pot to the table. "Actually it's ground chicory root but it makes a fair substitute."

He raised his cup for her to fill and took a sip. Grimacing he shook his head. "Whoa, do you have any sugar?"

Jenny pulled a dark clay jar from the shelf and removed the lid. "It's maple sugar but it'll cut the bitterness."

He stirred two chunks of the clumped brown sweetener into the cup, watching them dissolve before he took another sip. "Better," he said. "You drink this all the time."

Jenny smiled. "It's an acquired taste."

They dug into the eggs, supplementing them with the warm biscuits slathered with sweet butter they scooped from a small bowl centered on the table.

"This tastes okay but how come the butter's white?" Robert asked.

Jenny laughed. "You really are a city-boy. Butter is white. Companies put food coloring in it to make it yellow."

Robert shook his head. "Why?" Jenny shrugged.

Milo finished his third biscuit and looked at Jenny, cocking his head. She nodded then said, "Feed the chickens and make sure Rosie's okay before you go." The boy bounded to his feet and ran out the door.

"Where's he going?" Robert asked.

"He has some snares set in the woods. Checking them is usually the first thing he does every morning." She rose and gathered up her plate and Milo's. "I sent him out to see what he could find about how you got here, so he's a bit behind schedule."

Robert picked up his plate and followed her to the sink. He deposited it atop the ones Jenny had placed there then went back for the cups. He hesitated, sighed. "I may regret this, but is there more chicory?"

Jenny nodded toward the stove. "Help yourself."

He filled the cup, added a substantial chunk of maple sugar and drank the mix, punctuating the swallows with audible shudders that made Jenny grin. By the time he'd drained the brew, she had finished washing the breakfast dishes. She motioned for his cup. When he handed it to her, their fingers touched for an instant, and she flinched.

She turned her back on him and rinsed out the cup. Taking a deep breath, she straightened and faced him. "Let's see if we can find you a better place to bunk." She wiped her hands on the dishtowel and headed for the door. Robert followed.

"You know, I'm fine in here," he said when they entered the shed.

Jenny looked at him. Seeing he was serious she shrugged. "At least, we should be able to set up a better bed for you. Come with me." Outside, she walked quickly toward the large barn. In the far corner, she hauled out five straw bales from the pile and placed them on a small wagon. "Grab the handle while I steady the load." Robert pulled the wagon to the tool shed door then stood, eyes questioning.

"We'll tie them together lying on their side and cover them with one of the blankets," she explained. "It should make a pretty comfortable bed." They went to work removing the makeshift pallet and roping the bales together.

Robert stretched out on the new bed. "You're right, it is pretty comfortable." He got up. "Here, try it."

"No thanks," Jenny said backing toward the door.

"Oh, I ... that's not what I ..." he stammered, but she waved him off.

"It's okay," she said and left the shed. Outside she hurried toward her fenced garden, grabbed a hoe on the way through the gate, and busied herself cultivating the young snap beans.

Milo returned a half-hour later carrying two dead rabbits by their ears, blood dripping from the slashes he'd

16

made when he gutted them. He lashed them to the crossbar at the far end of the clotheslines, pulled his knife and skinned them. Jenny watched him work, admiring the economy of his skillful cuts. In what seemed like no time, he walked toward her grinning with the skins in his hands.

"Nice work, boy. Tack them up." His smile widened as he veered off toward the drying board on the south side of the barn. She became concerned that Robert had not come out of the tool shed since she'd left him there. "When you're done you can go tell Mr. Robert we're having rabbit stew for dinner."

Milo finished tacking the pelts to the board then ran to the tool shed and burst through the door. A few seconds later he walked out, head down. "He's sleepin'."

Jenny dropped her hoe and ran to the shed. Robert lay face up on his new bed, his breathing deep and regular, an erection bulging his trousers. She closed the door.

Chapter 3

Over the next few days, Milo's snares yielded six more rabbits. Jenny salted and dried strips of meat from three of them. She sent Milo down the hill with one carcass and a list of supplies for Jethro to buy in town. Later that morning, Jenny retrieved an onion and two potatoes from the root cellar. She cut some of her asparagus and put water on to boil. Grabbing a knife and large bowl, she went outside, took the last two rabbits over to the butchering block and beheaded them. She boned and trimmed the headless carcasses, cubed the meat and dropped it in the bowl. Back inside, she browned the meat in the skillet then dumped it into boiling water along with cut up vegetables, salt and some herbs. She moved the pot to a cooler part of the stovetop and went outside.

On her way to the garden, she saw Milo and Robert standing near the drying pelts. Milo was gesturing with his knife, startling her until she realized he was describing how to skin a rabbit. She stood for a time watching them. Soon Milo sensed that he was being watched. He stopped talking and turned to look at Jenny. She smiled at the enjoyment evident on his face and his lack of wariness. He returned the smile. Robert, seeing that the boy's attention was no longer on the skins, turned and saw her just as she removed the smile. He nodded and turned back to Milo, pointing at the place where the pelt had been severed from the rabbit's forefoot.

Jenny went back to her garden. She worked until she figured the stew was ready. Inside, she tasted the brew, thickened it with a little flour stirred into the mixture, and put the lid on the pot. Ten minutes later she called the two in for dinner.

"Wonderful stew, Jenny," Robert said, sopping up the dregs with one of the morning's leftover biscuits. "Milo, you're quite a trapper."

18

The boy grinned, nodded then noticing Jenny's frown, said, "Thank you Mr. Robert." Sitting up suddenly, eyes wide, he added, "Ya wanna see the snares?"

"I guess so," Robert answered. "How many do you have?"

Jenny watched Milo squint his eyes almost shut, head bobbing and fingers marking time while he counted. "Sebbenteen."

Robert glanced at Jenny, who shrugged. "Well, I guess I can go see some of them," he said.

The two slid their chairs back in unison. They took their plates to the sink and hurried out the door, leaving Jenny alone at the table. She rose and cleared the rest of the dishes. At the window above the sink, she watched them disappear into the woods, Milo animated, Robert nodding.

"What am I going to do with you," she mumbled, shaking her head.

Milo and Robert returned two hours later. Jenny watched from her perch on the corner of the porch as they emerged from the woods laughing, Robert looking sweaty and disheveled.

"Maw!" Milo shouted when he spied her. "Mr. Robert done learned how to build a snare."

She smiled at them. "Looks like he might have gotten himself caught in one."

"I kind of slipped out near the marsh," he shrugged. "I'm pretty much dry by now though."

Jenny stood. "If I recall right, there's an old pair of coveralls in that locker in the corner of the tool shed. Check and see if it fits and bring your clothes out so we can clean them up. Also," she pointed to the barn, "there's a pump, a basin and probably a bar of soap in the

19

springhouse around behind the barn. Looks like you could use a little cleaning up, too." She gestured to the boy, "Milo, you show him."

"Thanks, Jenny," Robert said. "No need to bother Milo, I think I can find my way to the other side of the barn." He headed for the tool shed. "I think I'll check out those coveralls first."

Milo ran past her into the house, emerging a minute later with his arithmetic book. "Mr. Robert said he'd show me the ma … math-a-matics about makin' a snare." He picked up Jenny's brief frown immediately. "That okay, Maw?"

"Of course it is," she said, patting his shoulder. "Mr. Robert will be out in a minute."

The boy plopped himself down on the porch facing the tool shed. Jenny remained standing beside him. She noticed that everything had stopped to wait for Robert, and that concerned her. He came out a moment later wearing the light brown oil-stained coveralls, sleeves and pant-legs rolled up several inches and the crotch of the garment riding slightly above his knees.

"Looks like whoever wore these was a bit bigger than me."

Nodding, Jenny left Milo sitting on the porch and walked toward Robert.

He approached awkwardly, his soiled clothes bundled under his arm. "Where can I wash these?"

"Give them to me." She said. "I have to wash things for Milo and me anyway."

"Are you sure?"

"Give." She held out her arms. He handed her the bundle with a grateful smile. "Milo is waiting for you to explain the finer mathematical points of snare-making."

20

She nodded toward the boy waiting on the porch then pivoted on her heel and headed for the wash platform next to the garden.

Jenny tossed Robert's clothing on top of Milo's then gathered her own from the porch. She shaved some soap from an irregular shaped bar into the tub full of sun-warmed water then swirled the clothes around until the soap had mostly dissolved. She worked each piece on the scrub board. An hour later, the last article of clothing hung on the line to dry, she tipped both the wash and rinse tubs into a trough that directed the water to the garden. Wiping her pruned hands on her dress, she pressed them against the small of her back, arching her body into them.

The sound of Milo's laughter led her toward the front of the cabin. Stopping at the corner, Jenny peaked around the wall. Robert and Milo were on their knees, drawing in the red dirt. She approached their workplace. "What's up with you two?"

The boy and man looked up simultaneously, smiles broad on their dirt-streaked faces. "We're designing the best snare in the world," Robert offered.

"Yeah, Maw. We got one where the rabbit gets in but can't get out."

"Milo, I think that describes any snare."

"Yeah, but this'un lets the critter walk aways to get into the food then it gets lost trying to leave." He pointed to the dirt. "Come see!"

Jenny walked up beside Milo and looked at the complicated mass of stick-drawn lines covering several square feet of the front yard. "Hmm, looks like a maze."

"Exactly," Robert chimed in. "The victim enters this confusing set of hallways to reach the bait then can't find its way out."

"Ain't it great?"

"Well, it certainly is exotic, but I think there's a problem."

"Whut?" Milo's face clouded.

"Wouldn't the rabbit just backtrack on its own scent trail and walk out?"

"Ah, Jenny. You have no faith in our genius," Robert said. "As soon as the varmint reaches the bait and takes a nibble it trips a lever that flips several walls sideways - Here …here … and here." He pointed a long stick at the key spots in their design then sat back on his heels. "… thus trapping the critter in an endless loop." He and the boy grinned up at Jenny.

"Well, I can't deny that it could work." She shook her head, grinning. "However, I don't think there's enough lumber on the farm to build it."

Milo laughed. "We was only funnin', Maw. We ain't really gonna build it." He pointed at an arrangement of numbers in the dust on the far side of the diagram. "Mr. Robert wus explainin' the math-a-matics of it."

"Ah," she looked at Robert. "I guess I'd best leave you two alone then."

He smiled up at her then turned toward Milo and continued amplifying their design. Jenny watched for a few more seconds before turning toward the cabin, a worried frown clouding her face.

Inside, she leaned on the table shaking her head in a slow pendulum motion. "I can't." She bit her lip and sat hard on the nearest chair. "What am I going to do with you?"

Chapter 4

Well after sundown Milo and Robert entered the cabin, their arms caked with red dust. Jenny ladled out the rest of the stew that had been simmering on the stove while they cleaned up at the sink, one pumping while the other washed. She put a loaf of sourdough on the table and sat, waiting for them to finish.

"How is the snare design going?" she asked when they joined her.

"We ran into a snag," Robert said. She cocked her head waiting.

"Yeah, we done run outta yard. Couldn't draw no more without cuttin' some trees or movin' the cabin." Milo's mischievous grin made her laugh out loud and the other two joined her.

After dinner, Milo went out to bed down the chickens and check on Rosie. Jenny sent Robert to the clothesline to check the laundry while she rinsed the dishes. When Milo returned, he said a quick good night to Jenny and climbed up to his loft. Within minutes Jenny heard his deep rhythmic breathing. Robert entered, dressed in his own clothes and looking free of the red dust. Jenny motioned him to the porch before he'd had a chance to close the door. She followed him out then turned and walked to the far corner, sitting on the plank floor with her bare feet dangling over the edge. He sat beside her about a foot away.

"Seems to me you're well enough to be thinking about going home." She looked at him and, seeing he was about to speak, hurried on. "I'll send Milo over the Jethro's tomorrow. He can bring his truck up and drive you where you need to go."

"Jenny, I ..."

23

"He can take you all the way to Arkville and you can catch a train or bus from there."

"Jenny ..."

"I hope you'll be okay. It can be a terrible thing to be robbed. You ..." Robert slapped his hand on the plank floor causing Jenny to jump.

"Jenny, stop. Please." She chewed her lip, not looking at him. "I ..." She waited for him to continue. After an uncomfortable silence, he added, "Everything I owned was in my car."

"Your car?"

"Yeah, I guess that went with whoever took my wallet and watch."

"What about family?" she tried. "There must be somebody who's looking for you?"

"I'm an only child and both my parents are gone." He shook his head. "I'm it."

They stared into the night, separated by converging thoughts and two six-inch wide planks.

"Milo's a great kid," Robert said, keeping his eyes on the starry sky. Jenny waited, hoping he wouldn't continue, knowing he would. "It's curious, though. I mean he's so backwoods hillbilly and you, his mother - you're ... well, sophisticated, educated. It's like you don't belong to the same world, much less the same family." Jenny hopped off the porch and hurried toward the barn. Robert ran to catch up with her, grabbing her arm. She wrenched free and turned, eyes angry.

"What I am to Milo and he to me are none of your business!" She glared at him as she continued. "We saved your damned life and now you need to pry into ours. What kind of person are you?"

Robert backed up a step, palms raised in front of him. "I thank you for that, I really do. It's just that you two are so very different. I can't make sense of it."

"Why do you need to?"

"I like Milo." He stepped toward her and she stiffened. "I ... I like you both." He reached for her arm but she pulled back. "What is it? Why are you so afraid?"

"I don't know you. I don't know if your name's really Robert or where you come from or anything about you except you have those shrapnel wounds." She paced back and forth, not looking at him as she spoke. "You haven't told me anything ... about you." She stopped, facing him, arms folded across her breasts.

"I come from Glenwood, Minnesota. Born April 30, 1952 - 7 pounds 8 ounces, my mother said - graduated from the central school in 1970 and joined the army. By August I was in Vietnam and by September I was in a VA Hospital in Hawaii with my head wrapped in a lot of white gauze and hurting like hell." He leaned against the barn door. "I left the hospital in June of '71 with a disability pension and assurances that the metal piece in my head wouldn't cause me any trouble." He let out a short laugh. "I went to college on the GI Bill, graduating with a master's degree in mathematical analysis and a job at West Virginia Junior College in Morgantown. I left there after six years because it was clear I wouldn't be tenured. I've never been married, not that I haven't thought about it." He spread his arms. "Anything else? Oh, yeah. My full name is Lars Robert Gunderson."

Jenny hadn't moved but her expression had softened. "Where were you going?"

He frowned. "I had two interviews lined up in Tallahassee. I decided to take a scenic route." He shoved his hands into his trouser pockets. "Now it's your turn."

Milo's Gift

"No," she said turning toward the cabin. "It's not."

Chapter 5

Jenny parried Robert's inquiries for the next several days, until he finally stopped questioning her. She didn't buy his story about a scenic route to Tallahassee for a minute, but she also didn't much care about the lie. She was getting used to having him around and it worried her. Robert would complicate their lives if he stayed, but Milo … Milo was drawn to him.

The next morning after Milo returned from running his snare line, the three sat down to a buckwheat pancake breakfast with maple syrup and blueberry preserves. Shoveling a large bite of pancake into his mouth, Milo asked, "Mr. Robert, want to see where you wus brought in?"

"That would be great, Milo."

"That okay, Maw?" Jenny nodded.

When the two left, she cleaned the dishes, pulled in the rest of yesterday's laundry, then sat on her bed to sort and fold. She heard Jethro's old International Scout rattling up the coal road a minute before it came into view and went out to meet it. The silver-haired giant pulled his six and a half foot frame out of the Scout and stretched. "These old bones get a might creaky nowadays, Miss Jenny."

"You'll outlive us all Jethro," she said as she reached him. "Did you get my flour?"

"Sure did." He reached into the back of the truck. Hauling out a twenty-five pound sack of flour, he swung it effortlessly to his shoulder then retrieved a bag with an assortment of other supplies before turning to face Jenny. "Your flour bin empty?"

"I used up the last of it this morning."

The big man nodded and walked past her into the cabin. Jenny followed. He emptied the flour sack into the large ceramic barrel and replaced the lid. Jenny unloaded the other bag.

Supplies stowed, they walked out to the truck together, Jenny's arm hooked in his. The old man's huge scarred hand clamped on the door handle but didn't open it. He turned toward Jenny.

"Anything wrong, Jethro?"

"I been troubled some this past week, Miss Jenny."

"About what?"

"I mighta done something wrong. I … I just ain't sure about it."

She rested her hand over his on the door handle. "You want to tell me about it?" He looked down at her, took a deep breath and nodded. "Let's go sit on the porch." She guided him back to the cabin and hoisted herself up to her perch on the end of the porch, bare feet dangling. He sat beside her examining the grime on the knuckles of his right hand. "Tell, Jethro," she urged.

Another deep breath and he started, "Last week, I wus on m'way to Arkville fer supplies 'n they wus a dead body just at the edge of the coal road. Mighta missed it 'cept a red fox run cross the county road right in front of me 'n I had to stop. Watchin' her head into the woods I spied somethin' so I got out to see." Jethro's broad left hand teased his long white beard while he spoke. "He wadn't breathin' 'n I didn't wanna haul him into Arkville. They's folks there woulda thought I'd kilt him." He turned toward Jenny and cocked his head. "I didn't though."

"I know." She stroked his massive arm. "Go on."

"Well, I was goin' to town 'n couldn't take him, so alls I could think of wus t' hide him somewhere till I could come back 'n bury him proper." Jethro nodded his head,

28

as if agreeing with himself. "I carried him into the wood aways, to skunk holler. I put him down on the ridge, I did. I guess it wus a might too close to the edge though, cause he rolled down 'n lit right near the creek - arms spread like Jesus they wus." He shook his head, grinning, then his face turned serious and he continued. "I went back next mornin' to haul'm up and bury him but he wus gone. I think mebbe some big ole boar drug him off, or somethin'. Don't make sense though. Not a bit." He shook his head. "I shoulda took time to bury him."

Jenny sat quiet for a moment then said, "Good thing you didn't, Jethro. He wasn't dead."

Jethro turned to face her so quickly he almost slid off the porch. "Whut? But he wadn't breathin' I ..." His face clouded and he looked away head down.

"Milo found him, must have been shortly after you left. He was in a deep coma. We brought him here and he woke up a couple of hours later. He and Milo are out in the woods right now." She looked up and, seeing his confusion was about to explain the word 'coma' but another thought occurred to her. She slid off the porch, turning to face the man who slouched head down, his hands worrying each other in his lap. "Jethro, look at me please." Slowly he raised his head, eyes darting to either side before settling on her face. "Jethro, do you have the man's wallet?"

His bearded chin moved as if trying to help him form uncomfortable words. His head cocked toward his right shoulder. "Miss Jenny, I thought it'd be okay. Didn't figure he'd need nothin' like that, bein' dead like he ..." He stopped, head down.

She nodded. "Do you still have it?" He nodded toward the truck. "Show me." Jenny strode toward the vehicle with the big man shuffling behind. She stepped aside to let him pass when they got close. He opened the door and climbed in, reaching across to the doorless glove compartment. Straightening with an audible grunt, Jethro handed her the wallet and a wristwatch with a Speidel band. Jenny slipped the watch over her wrist and opened the wallet. The West Virginia driver's license verified his name, with a Morgantown address. A photo of a tall angular man in front of a small white house, arm around the shoulders of a short woman, another of a large hound sitting beside a young boy, were the only other contents. The wallet contained no money. Holding the empty wallet open she faced Jethro.

"Miss Jenny, I figured he wadn't needin' money where he wus goin'." Responding to her deepening frown he added, "I done spent most of it. They wus about sebbenty dollar. I bought me a couple shirts ... 'n a sangwich at Missy's."

His expression reminded Jenny of a puppy caught chewing a shoe and she had to stifle a laugh. "It's okay, Jethro." She patted his shoulder. "Thank you for bringing my supplies. I'll send Milo down next month with a list. You go on home now." She swung the door shut and waited until he'd started the engine and drove across the yard to the coal road before returning to the porch. She opened the wallet and stared at the two photos for several minutes before removing both from the plastic sleeves. Placing the open wallet on the plank floor beside her, she turned them over and set them on her lap. *Eldred and Mary, June 1948* was written in light blue ink at an upward angle on the photo of the couple. The other was inscribed *Lars and Thor, July 1959 at Lake Minnewaska.*

Jenny returned the photos to their plastic sleeves, folded the wallet and slipped the watch from her wrist, placing the wallet inside the expansion band. Raising her legs until her knees almost reached her chin, she pivoted and planted her feet on the porch then stood and walked inside. She slid the wallet and watch under the corner of her mattress then set about preparing a meal. While she worked she let the new information about Robert roll around in her head.

Chapter 6

Milo and Robert emerged from the woods late in the afternoon, their faces showing signs of a lunchtime berry orgy. Milo ran ahead, bounding up the steps and through the door, planting both hands on the table to stop his forward motion. "Maw, did you know you c'n say how tall a tree is just by knowin' how tall you are your own self 'n how fur you are from the tree?"

"That so?" Jenny glanced over her shoulder while she stirred seasonings into her vegetable soup.

"Yup. Wanna see how?" He poised on the balls of his feet.

"Can it wait until after dinner?"

Disappointment crossed the boy's face. "I reckon."

Jenny put her wooden spoon aside and moved the large pot away from the hottest part of the stove. "I guess we have enough time," she said.

Milo grabbed her hand and hurried out the door and down the porch steps, head turning side to side. "Over there." He hurried toward the lone loblolly pine at the corner of Rosie's meadow, stopping some distance away. He dropped to the ground on his belly, made an awkward looking triangle with one thumb along the ground and the other pointing down so that their tips touched and made about a ninety-degree angle, sliding his forefinger up then down until it touched the base of the down-pointing thumb, he tried to sight along it. He scooted back several feet, duplicated the move then forward a foot and triangulated a third time and smiled. "You stand here." He knelt and drew an 'X'. Jenny put her left foot on top of the 'X', drawing her right foot up next to it. Lying down with his feet touching Jenny's and his head pointing at the tree, Milo marked that spot with a

32

line. He stood and took a long stride, looked at his leg spread and took another as close as he could to the length of the first. He repeated the process until his last, shorter step brought him up to the base of the tree. "That wus twennie-one and a bit more than half another." He ran back to where Jenny stood, dropped to his knees and wrote the number '21' in the dirt then 'x3' under it. With his tongue prominently displayed between his lips, he made the calculation writing '63' below it. "Gotta add the extra," he said, writing '2' under his result and, finally '65' under that. "The pine's sixty-five feet tall," he said with great confidence.

"Did you add your body length?" Robert's voice close behind Jenny startled her causing her to move from her position in Milo's measurement scheme. She turned to face him. Robert looked past her, adding, "You know how tall you are so all you have to do is add that to your result and you've got it."

Jenny turned back toward the boy in time to see his disappointment fade, replaced by a bright-eyed smile. He dropped to his knees, wrote '6' under his last calculation and finished the sum with the number '71'.

"That's got'er." Milo nodded, rising and facing the adults. "I make it sebbenty-one feet."

"Very good, but you're not six feet tall, you're about five-nine." Jenny said.

"Mr. Robert says, ah kin round up on stuff 'cus I'm kinda close."

"Good work," Robert added, stepping up beside her.

Grinning, Milo looked from one to the other and back. Jenny smiled and nodded. "Well, boy, if you don't need me anymore I have soup to tend to." She turned toward the cabin. "Dinner in about half an hour," she added without looking back.

They sat down to the evening meal just as the sun rested above Wylie's Mountain. Jenny served the vegetable soup into three bowls and placed a loaf of sourdough in the center of the table. "Eat up, there's plenty."

Robert dipped his spoon into the bowl, retrieving steaming chunks of potato, onion, and kale in a thin broth. He blew on it a few times then took it into his mouth and chewed. "Mmm. This is great. What's that interesting flavor? Kind of like an Italian thing."

"Fennel," Jenny answered unable to suppress a smile. "It is used in Italian cooking, sometimes."

"Are you Italian?" Jenny left the question unanswered. Robert shrugged and tore a piece off the loaf, dipping it into the soup.

Milo stopped eating and looked at Jenny, puzzled. "Whut's it mean? I-talian … to be that, I mean."

Jenny put down her spoon. "You remember all those countries we saw in the atlas?" The boy nodded. "One of them was Italy, it looked like a boot sticking out in the water, about ready to kick an island. Do you remember the name of the island?" Milo squinted then shook his head. "It's Sicily. Anyway, people who come from Italy are called Italians."

Milo nodded and went back to his soup.

"We'll talk more about it during our next geography lesson," Jenny said. "Now finish your meal and tend to the evening chores."

Milo ate quickly, put his dishes in the sink and bounded outside.

"Did Milo show you where you were brought into the hollow?" Jenny asked as she reached for his empty bowl.

"He says he did, but I couldn't see any of what he was pointing out as the trail." Robert shook his head. "We ended up at the edge of the woods where a dirt road he called 'The Coal Road' ended at a paved one."

Jenny stood at the sink, barely breathing while he spoke. "Sometimes Milo's imagination is better than his tracking," she offered.

"Maybe, but he seemed certain that we were standing in the spot where I'd been found. He even mentioned Jethro again." Robert rose and stood by the door. "Who is this Jethro?"

"He's an old gentleman that helps out here from time to time."

"To hear Milo talk, he sounds like a cross between Santa Clause and the Jolly Green Giant."

Jenny laughed. "That's not a bad description. Jethro's a big man."

"I'd like to meet him, sometime," Robert said. "He sounds ..." The door flew open smacking him full on the back and sending him toppling over his chair.

Milo stood in the doorway, eyes wide. "You alright Mr. Robert?" He moved quickly, kneeling by the man's side. "I sure didn't mean t' hurt ya."

Jenny dropped to her knees on his other side. Robert looked up smiling. t"I guess it's bad practice standing in front of a door." He used the side of the overturned chair to right himself, then rose to his feet. The other two rose with him. "Nothing seems broken." He moved arms and legs, flexing the various joints. "And, if I'm not dreaming, I appear to be conscious and relatively coherent." He turned to face Milo. "So, I guess I'm alright." He put an arm on the boy's shoulder. "I'd like it if you slowed down a little on your way through the door, though." Milo nodded, a sheepish grin on his face.

35

Jenny stood a pace away, observing her reaction to the possible injury to this man. Her fear when she saw him fall troubled her. She tried to convince herself that it was a perfectly normal emotion in that situation. She'd have been afraid, she thought for any person falling like that. True enough, another part of her brain answered, but there was something else, something she couldn't, or didn't want to, put her finger on. Her ruminations ceased when she saw Robert rubbing his left shoulder. "Let me see," she said approaching quickly.

"It's fine. Just a little bump."

"Milo, get me some bark from that witch hazel, the one by the edge of the path. Make it about twice the size of your hand." The boy hurried out the door. "Take off your shirt."

"But I'm fine, really."

"Just do it." He pulled the polo shirt over his head, leaving him in his undershirt, its straps bracketing his collarbone.

Milo reentered, opening the door with care. He held a slice of bark with the tips of two fingers. Jenny took it from him. Holding it by the edges she set it down and nodded for him to cut a length of twine from the roll hanging on the wall peg to the right of the stove. She showed him the length by spreading her hands. When he brought it to her she picked up the bark and shaped it on Robert's shoulder as best she could then secured it with the twine and the strap of his undershirt.

"That tingles," he said. "It feels really strange."

"It will keep the swelling down. Keep it on."

"How long?"

"Until morning."

Robert frowned. "How am I supposed to sleep?" Jenny shrugged and went back to the sink to finish the dishes. She heard the door open and close.

Chapter 7

Jenny was up before dawn the following morning. She dressed, tied an apron with a large front pocket over her dress and went outside to gather eggs. On her way back to the cabin she saw Milo emerge from the woods, brow furrowed. She met him at the steps.

"Maw, c'n I use the gun?"

Her pulse quickened. "What for?"

"I got a skunk in one a the snares." Milo shrugged. "He just hangin' there. I can't git'm down 'thout gettin' skunked."

Jenny looked at the boy's embarrassed grin. "Stay here," she ordered. Spinning on her heel, she hurried to the barn. At the door, she glanced over her shoulder. Seeing that he hadn't changed position, she stepped inside. On tiptoe she searched with her fingers until she found the key. Across the barn at a locked feed bin, she fitted the key and opened it. She unrolled an oiled canvas wrapping on top of another, much larger wrapped bundle, revealing a long-barreled Winchester single-shot .22. She wiped the rifle with a dry rag and removed the bolt. Checking that the barrel was clear, she reached in and opened a small green box, three-quarters full of Remington long-rifle hollow point shells. Withdrawing two, she closed and secured the box, closed and locked the bin, and returned the key to the shelf. She slipped the cartridges into her apron pocket with the nine eggs, slid the rifle bolt home and returned to the front porch and Milo.

"I have to take the eggs inside," she said handing him the rifle. "Hold this." Milo ran his hands along the dark walnut stock, petting it as one would a lounging cat. Jenny entered the cabin, put the eggs in a large bowl. "Show me," she ordered when she returned.

They walked a half mile or so southwest to the edge of a clearing where a fat skunk dangled by a hind leg about four feet off the ground. Jenny and Milo circled the animal until she raised her hand. "See how that tree trunk is just a short way behind it? We always need to make sure of the background before shooting."

Milo frowned like she'd said something stupid. "Paw taught that. Remember?"

Jenny shivered slightly and nodded. "Sorry. You sure you can do a clean head shot? We don't want it to suffer any more."

"Uh huh."

Jenny reached into her apron and retrieved one of the shells. Milo stretched out on the ground in a perfect prone firing position, opened the bolt and put his palm up without taking his eyes off the animal. Jenny dropped the shell into his hand, and watched while he shoved it into the chamber and slid the bolt home. He pulled the cocking knob straight back. Jenny heard the click when it reached full cock. Milo sighted on his target, drew in his breath, expelled some of it and squeezed the trigger. The sharp crack of the shot, accompanied almost immediately by the hole appearing in the skunk's skull and the thunk of the spent bullet burying itself into the trunk, made Jenny aware that she'd been holding her breath also. She let it go with an audible sigh. "Nice shot, boy."

He cleared the weapon and handed it back to Jenny then picked up the empty shell and stood. He walked slowly toward the swinging carcass, wary of any possible movement. When he reached it, he released the skunk, letting it fall to the ground and slid it out of the way with his foot. In a minute he had the mechanism reset and baited. He picked up the skunk and turned toward Jenny. "Whut should I do with it?"

"Skin it, I'd say. Be careful of the scent glands."
She left him there, retracing their path back to the cabin.
When she cleared the woods, Robert was sitting on the
porch eating scrambled eggs and drinking chicory. When
he saw the rifle his eyes narrowed.

"You been hunting?" he said, eyes locked on the
weapon.

"No," she answered and walked past him on her
way to the barn. He hopped off the porch and fell in step
with her. She stopped. "Go back to the porch and wait."

"Why?"

"Because if you follow me I might be inclined to
shoot you. Get me a cup of that stuff. I'll be right back."
She watched him turn and walk toward the cabin before
continuing into the barn where she stored the weapon and
cartridge. When she returned he was sitting on the porch
holding a steaming cup of brew out to her. She took it,
sipped and sat against the corner post.

"What was going on out there?" he asked.

"Milo trapped a skunk. He had to shoot it."

"Why all the secrecy about the gun?" Jenny took
another sip but didn't answer. He looked like he was about
to ask again when Milo emerged holding the skunk's
beautiful black and white pelt.

"Wanna help me tack it, Mr. Robert?"

The man slid off the porch. "Sure." He followed
the boy toward the south side of the barn.

Watching them disappear around the corner, Jenny
shivered and took another swallow. In a few minutes they
reappeared, separating at the center of the yard, Robert
toward the outhouse, and Milo to her perch on the porch.
He stopped close in front of her, head down.

40

"What's wrong, boy?" she lifted his chin and was struck by the profound sadness she saw. "Milo?"

"I wisht I hadn'ta had t' shoot him." Jenny let out her breath and most of her tension.

"There wasn't anything else you could do," she said. "Sometimes you have to do bad things for good reasons." She stroked his cheek; he leaned his head into her touch.

Milo straightened, his expression now determined. He made eye contact. "I gotta think on it some."

Jenny knew that look. She hesitated only a moment then nodded and slid off the porch, wrapping him in her arms. "Be careful."

Milo returned the embrace briefly then stepped backward and in a moment disappeared into the forest.

"Where's Milo going?" Robert asked from close behind her.

Jenny started. "Dammit! Could you make a little more noise when you come up behind me." She looked over her shoulder.

"Should I stomp my feet, or whinny, or maybe moo?" He was smiling.

She glared and turned her attention back to where Milo had melted into the woods.

"Well?"

"Well what?"

Where's he going?"

She returned to the porch and her cold drink before answering. "He wants to come to terms with the killing."

What killing?"

She stared at the man. "The skunk, of course. Milo only kills for food. It troubles him that he had to kill the skunk."

Robert lifted himself onto the porch next to her. "I was thinking about asking him to show me some more of his wood lore." He shrugged. "I guess it can wait till this afternoon."

Jenny shook her head. "Not likely. He'll probably be gone a couple of days. He was last time."

"You mean you let him wander off like that?"

"I don't 'let him'. When it comes to things like this he doesn't ask; he informs me that he's leaving."

"But aren't you worried?"

Jenny glanced over to the woods. "No, ... well yes. But not that he'll get lost or starve. He'll be fine that way."

Robert nodded, followed her gaze. "Where does he go?"

"I have no idea." Jenny shrugged. "He's been doing it ever since ... for years. It's his way of sorting out things." She lifted herself from the porch and dropped to the ground raising small dust clouds at her feet. "I wish we'd get some rain." She walked into the cabin, leaving Robert on the porch, his eyes on the woods.

When Jenny emerged, chewing on a hunk of buttered bread, she saw the tool shed door swing shut. She walked to the lean-to that sheltered their firewood, reaching it just as she popped the last bite into her mouth. Wiping her hands on her dress, she reached for a maple log about two feet long and a foot in diameter, lugged it to the chopping block, and set it on end. She picked up the heavy splitting maul. Planting her feet wide apart, she swung the maul over her head and divided the log in half. She retrieved one of the halves and split it then did the same with the other. She stacked the pieces on the small

42

iron-wheeled wagon they'd used for the straw bales then went back to the pile for another log.

She'd positioned the new log for the first cut when she heard "Moo!" coming from the middle of the yard. Laughing, she turned toward the sound. "Permission to come aboard. Moo!" He stood at attention holding a salute until she returned it then he strode up to the chopping block. "Let me do this," he said, picking up the maul.

"Do you know how?" Jenny asked, backing out of swinging distance.

"Contrary to popular opinion, there are trees in Minnesota." He raised the maul and halved the log with a perfectly placed blow. "And we damn sure had wood stoves." He picked up a half and placed it on the block.

"Okay, enjoy yourself." She walked to the barn, grabbed a basket and dropped a small trowel into it. "I'm going to do a little foraging," she called on her way toward the Wylie Mountain path. He waved an arm without looking then continued working.

Jenny located the game trail several feet into the woods, checked the sun position and turned right. Within a half hour she'd gathered a stew quantity of oyster mushrooms and a cluster of wine-caps. She veered off the game trail when it intersected a wider path that led home by way of a marshy area. In the marsh, she cut some young jewelweed to add to her basket. She continued foraging, always moving in the general direction of the cabin. Suddenly she stopped. The familiar surroundings startled her. She'd avoided the area all these years during her foraging expeditions, had wished it out of existence. She froze, knowing, now that she stood within yards of the place, that she had to enter. The basket nearly fell from her hand. The act of catching it somehow freed her to take a step and then the next, until she reached the broad sandy clearing with the shallow pit gouged out dead center.

She approached the pit, her steps slow, deliberate, heel and toe, heel and toe, until both feet came together at the rim. The ashes of the burned carcasses had mixed with the sand over the years until the bottom of the pit was a series of gray-brown streaks with dead oak leaves scattered in random patterns among them. "You always had to burn them," she mumbled, remembering how he'd skin the animal and butcher it, placing what he called 'the good parts' into the galvanized tub. He made her haul the heavy tub to the smokehouse, stumbling in the leather hobble tethering her ankles. The bad parts always got burned. Here. Her legs wouldn't hold her anymore and she dropped to her knees then sat back on her heels. She leaned forward and vomited into the pit.

The sun had rolled well into the afternoon sky before Jenny felt strong enough to move. Struggling to her feet, she picked up the basket and backed away from the pit and out of the sandy clearing. Once in the trees, she ran toward the cabin.

Jenny slowed to a walk just before she cleared the tree line. She watched as Robert brought the splitting maul up over his head ready to split another log. He was surrounded by what appeared to her to be half a cord of freshly split wood. His shirt and undershirt were hanging on a nail and sweat ran down his back, which she noticed had reddened from the sun. She continued into the cabin and stored the herbs, then set the mushrooms aside and put the jewelweed into a pot with water to boil. After she filled the kettle, put it on the stove and added wood to the fire, she sat on her bed, hands clutching her sides, and rocked back and forth. Tears traced ragged tracks down her dusty cheeks.

Robert backed through the door, arms loaded with fresh split maple. Pivoting around the open door he nudged it with his heel, concentrating on balancing the wood. As he stepped toward the wood box Jenny released a sob she'd been unable to contain. Robert's head snapped toward the sound. "Jenny! My God, what's wrong?"

He stared for a moment then hurried to the woodbox and dropped his armload, most of it missing its mark. He hurried across the room, knelt in front of her and put his hands on her shoulders. She raised her head and threw her arms around him, sliding to her knees and burying her face in his sweaty shoulder. "What is it?" he asked. "Are you hurt?" She shook her head against him. "Is it Milo?" She shook her head again. She felt his body relax.

They stayed that way, Jenny sobbing, Robert rubbing her back, until she felt like she had no strength left. Releasing her grip, she leaned back, started to speak then took his head in both hands and kissed him softly, tenderly at first then with increasing ferocity. Robert responded, wrapping his arms around her, pulling her close. They held the kiss until Jenny felt she could no longer breathe and broke it. When she tilted her head back to look at him he smiled and kissed the hollow at the base of her neck then her cheek. His hands explored her back, settling on her hips pulling her closer. She leaned back placing both hands on his chest, sliding them down to his belt, answering the question in his eyes.

Chapter 8

"You dropped the wood," Jenny said, as they lay side-by-side on the floor, naked bodies streaked with sweat and red dust.

"You left the kettle boiling."

Jenny stretched both arms above her head, touching the leg of the nearest chair, her body arched. She relaxed and rolled to a sitting position looking around for her dress. Locating it near the bed, she stretched her right foot until her toes clamped onto a piece of the thin fabric. She dragged it within arms reach and fumbled with it, finally sliding it over her head; she rose to let the fabric fall around her body.

Robert watched without moving. When she'd removed the kettle, carefully avoiding the scattered firewood, she turned to face him. "Fix the firewood." He sat up and reached for his trousers, slipped them on then fastened his belt. Piece by piece he deposited the wood in the near-empty woodbox.

Task completed, he sat in the nearest chair. "Why were you crying?"

She shook her head without turning around. "Not now."

He stood and put his hands on her shoulders. "When?"

"Not now." She leaned back against him. "Maybe soon." She straightened and turned, carrying a basin of water, a worn bar of soap floating in it. "You're filthy. Wash."

"You're no rosebud yourself," he said.

Jenny grinned and placed the basin on the table. "You first. Drop 'em."

Milo's Gift

Chapter 9

That night after the evening meal, Jenny pushed Robert out the door over his mild protests and watched while he shuffled across the yard trailed by his soft shadow in the moonlight. When the tool shed door closed she left the window and walked to her bed and sat. Reaching under the corner of the mattress she extracted the wallet and watch. She slid the watch off the worn leather and set them side-by-side on the bed. She picked up the watch, twisting and flexing the band. Turning it over, she thought she saw an inscription on the back but the glow from the distant candle wasn't bright enough to read it so she rose and approached the table. Sitting in the nearest chair, Jenny leaned forward and held the watch close to the flame. Squinting, she read the worn letters *ELG* and *5-6-19* but the rest of the number was unreadable. She returned to the bed and picked up the wallet, bringing it back to the candle. She pulled the photos out and reread the information on the back. "Must be his father's," she mused. Returning them to their plastic slots she folded the wallet. When she put it on the table next to the watch she noticed for the first time how it sagged, like the leather had once needed to contain a great deal more than two photos, a license and twenty dollars. *Could Jethro have lied about the amount of money?* she thought, but rejected the idea. She trusted the old man with every cent she had and he'd been honest and reliable. What then? What would make a wallet expand like that? Then she laughed, "Condoms, of course. Jethro, you old rascal."

Chapter 10

The next morning Jenny woke with a broad smile on her face. She teased the embers in the cook stove, added birch bark kindling and waited until it caught before tossing in two small splits of maple. She filled the kettle and placed it on the stove and mixed up some pancake batter while it heated. Outside her window the grayness of the cloudy dawn grew brighter. She spotted Rosie, neck stretched through the rail fence to reach some succulent weed that had caught her eye.

Jenny wondered where Milo was, more curious than worried. Once, a few years back, she tried to follow him but his speed and stealth in his element soon made her realize the futility of the endeavor. Her face clouded as she recalled, reluctantly, the first time he'd gone off after … She shook her head and bit her lip until it became the reason for the tears forming in her eyes. "Don't go back," She growled. "Don't."

The sight of the tool shed door opening and Robert, shirtless in the chill morning, heading for the outhouse brought her into the present. Her frown softened, watching his progress. She continued to stare until he came out of the facility and disappeared around the side of the barn. Feeling the smile on her face she mumbled, "Easy, girl." She set the pancake batter aside to rest then went to the pantry shelf and retrieved a jar of sliced peaches. Lifting the steaming kettle from the heat, she poured water into the coffee pot. She removed two adjacent lids from the stove and set the cast iron griddle over the holes then stoked the fire, adding another split. By the time Robert entered, there were four pancakes ready to be turned.

"Morning," he said, coming up behind her. He kissed her neck sending a chill down her body.

"Pancakes will be ready in a minute. Pour the coffee." She flipped the cakes then reached for the jar of peaches and opened it, placing it in the center of the table.

Robert put one filled cup at each place and sat. "Any word from Milo?" Jenny shook her head without turning. "And you have no idea where he goes?" Another head shake.

Jenny scooped two golden brown cakes from the griddle and slid them onto one of the plates then did the same with the other two cakes. She brought the plates to the table, placing one in front of Robert and the other at her place. As she scooped syrupy peach slices onto her pancakes, she frowned. "Robert?"

"Mmm?" He chewed the mouthful waiting for her to continue.

"What kind of car did you have?"

He swallowed, glanced away and finally answered, "Chevy," adding, "It was a rental car." He forked another mouthful of pancake into his mouth. "Why?"

Jenny's eyes locked on his. "You didn't get too upset when you found out it was gone and that made me curious." She sliced into her pancakes and swiped the forkful through a puddle of syrup before taking it to her mouth. She swallowed before adding, "But since the car didn't belong to you, I guess it makes some sense you weren't hysterical about losing it."

"You guess?" he responded. Jenny nodded. "Don't you believe me?" She shrugged and took another bite. Robert started to say something else then dropped his fork and left.

Jenny cleared the table. She poured hot water from the kettle into the dishpan, mellowed it with water from the pump and washed the dishes, wiping the occasional tear that escaped with her forearm. "I want to believe you,

Robert," she said, glancing out the window at the closed tool shed door.

After putting the last dish on the drain board, Jenny dried her hands and padded over to her bed. Sitting, she drew the wallet with the encircling watch from under the mattress, slipped the watch on her wrist and opened the wallet. She examined it, turning it over and over in her hands. She didn't know why, but the feel of the soft leather calmed her. The two photos and the license stared back at her from their respective plastic slots. The remaining empty compartments didn't appear to have ever contained anything, nor did the flip side of the occupied ones. The three items were in consecutive locations indicating to her that they sat in their original positions. "No credit card," she said, folding the wallet and sliding the watch from her wrist into its former position around the leather.

The rest of the day Jenny went about her chores avoiding Robert. When he came into the cabin around noon he found a plate with sourdough bread and venison jerky on the table and Jenny at the sink peeling beets. She didn't acknowledge his presence.

That evening she asked him to bring in more wood before they sat down to dinner. When he reentered, arms loaded with dry maple she had already put food on the table and was in her chair. He shoved the load into the woodbox and took his place. Jenny avoided looking at him, playing with the morsels on her plate until he'd eaten.

When he got up to leave, he said, "Goodnight." Jenny nodded.

Lying back on her bed later, she sighed, knowing what she had to do in the morning. "Be honest with me, Robert," she said, closing her eyes.

Chapter 11

Waking with the dawn, Jenny stoked the stove, put the kettle on to heat and stepped outside to watch the sunrise. It startled her to see Milo sitting, back against a porch railing, arms hugging his knees. "What's up, boy?"

"I ain't sure, Maw."

She sat beside him. "Talk."

He stared at the rising sun. Jenny waited.

Finally, with the little nod that always indicated he'd made his decision, Milo spoke. "I wus way over past the old Dickerson place, down by the big lake they built back when I wus little."

Jenny frowned. "That was pretty close to Arkville."

"Ain't nobody seen me, Maw. It's okay." He waited for her to relax before he continued. "Anyways, I heard folks aways off so I clumb a sycamore to get a better look." He gazed back toward the east then with a long breath, continued. "They was eight kids, even number a boys 'n girls, probly older 'n me, 'n they was swimmin'." He stopped again, scratched his head, shook it. "Thing is, they was nekkid."

Jenny smiled. "That's pretty normal, Milo."

Milo shook his head again. "I know. Thing is the girls, they had …" he frowned and pointed at Jenny.

"Breasts?" Milo nodded. "It's okay to say that," she offered. "So? Girls, after a certain age do get them."

"I know, Maw. You taught." He shook his head harder. "Thing is, I started feelin' real funny," he pointed to his crotch "down there."

Jenny chewed her lower lip. *You had to know this day would come* she thought. "Funny how?"

52

"Like I wanted to run down there n' grab them b...breasts. Like I wanted to put my hands all over they nekkid selfs."

"Uh huh," she nodded. "What about the boys?" she asked, more to buy time than out of any need to know.

Milo looked at her for a long moment before answering. "T'was like they didn't matter. I just wanted t' touch the girls."

Jenny's breath quickened. She laid a hand on his arm. "What did you do?"

"Jus' watched," he said. "Wouldn't a been right to do other."

Jenny smiled, relieved. "You did alright, Milo." She put her arm around him, pulling him close. He rested his head on her shoulder while they watched the morning brighten.

After a time, Jenny tousled Milo's hair. "Hungry?"

He nodded and stood. "But, I oughta check my snares."

"Eat first." He hesitated then smiled and headed inside.

Chapter 12

Milo was sopping up the last of his eggs with a biscuit when Robert came in. "Milo, good to see you," he said, sitting across from the boy. Milo smiled, rose, and bounded out the door. "Where's he going now?"

"Checking snares," Jenny said, sliding two fried eggs onto a plate. She placed it in front of Robert then sat.

"Aren't you eating?"

"I did." She watched him, her eyes never leaving his face.

Finally, he put his fork down. "What?"

"I want to trust you, Robert, I do. But you haven't been honest with me."

He looked quickly down at his plate then back at Jenny. "What do you mean?"

She rose and went to her bed, drew the wallet and watch from under the mattress. "There's no credit card in here 'Lars' and I believe you need one to rent a car." She returned to her seat, resting her elbows on the table, the wallet held in both hands. Her eyes never left his face.

He stared at her. "You said my pockets were empty when you found me."

"They were. Jethro had this." Jenny dropped his possessions in the middle of the table. "He was the one who carried you from the road. He was going to come back and bury you after he returned from town."

Robert shivered. He picked them up, slid the watch onto his wrist and caressed the soft leather wallet. "It feels empty."

"It pretty much is."

He opened it. Spreading the billfold, he frowned. "I had money in there."

Jenny's jaw tensed. "How much?"

Robert's brow wrinkled. "a fifty and a twenty."

She relaxed a little. "Jethro didn't think a dead man needed money so he took it. I think he bought lunch."

"With seventy bucks?"

"He's got a big appetite." She slapped her hands on the table. Robert flinched. "What about the car?"

Robert's tongue swept his lips, leaving them damp. He shook his head several times as if trying to clear it. His faced turned crimson. "I ... I lost it in a poker game in Huntington. I lost everything, except this stuff and the clothes I'm wearing." He sagged in the chair.

Jenny let his explanation roll around in her mind, all the time watching his face. Finally she said, "Why did you lie?"

He shrugged. "I don't know. I guess when I woke up I thought I still had everything ... that I'd been dreaming or something."

"At some point you must have realized it was no dream."

"After a while it didn't seem to matter."

Jenny frowned. "What do you mean?"

He fidgeted in his seat. "I ... Well I kind of liked being here and I was afraid that you'd want me to leave if I told you, after ..."

"... you lied?" she finished. Robert stood. "What are you doing?"

He turned toward the door. "I figure you probably want me to leave so I was going to pack."

"You've got nothing to pack."

"Yeah, you're right." He opened the door. "I do have to put my socks and shoes on, though." She looked at his feet, surprised she hadn't noticed they were bare.

Jenny let him leave. She thought over the story, believed it, and stood quickly, tipping the chair over. She hurried through the door. "Robert?" Halfway across the yard, he turned. "Where will you go?"

He shrugged. "I don't know."

"You have no money." He shrugged again.

Jenny chewed her lower lip. "Are you any good with a hammer?"

"My dad was a builder."

"I don't think it's genetic," she smiled.

"I helped out after school and summers."

She nodded. "I need some repair work done to the buildings on the farm," she nodded in the direction of her front door, "Including the house. I can pay you fifty-five dollars a week plus room and board."

"Fifty-five?"

"Plus room and board," she reminded him.

By the time Milo returned, Robert was reseating some loose boards at the corner of the barn, several nail heads protruding from his tight lips. He responded to Milo's "Howdy, Mister Robert" with a wave of his hammer and a nod.

Milo approached the garden where Jenny rested on her haunches, picking tomatoes and bell peppers for supper. "Nothin' today," he said.

She stood and pressed her hands against the small of her back. "Find me a big onion in the root cellar." She watched Milo lope toward the partially hidden earthen mound on the shaded side of the cabin and disappear behind it. He met her on the porch with a large Vidalia onion in his calloused hand.

"What's Mister Robert doin'?"

"He's working for me. I hired him as a handyman."

Milo smiled. "That mean he stayin'?"

"For the time being," Jenny answered, returning his smile.

"Reckon I'll go help," Milo said and hurried toward the barn.

Jenny watched him cross the yard, her smile fading. She carried her basket of vegetables into the house.

At the sink, she reexamined each item, rinsed it and set it on the counter. Watching the two work on the repairs, she thought about what the future might bring, whether Robert would be part of it, whether Milo would be okay as he grew, whether she could actually trust this man she knew so little about. "Give it time," she said. "More time."

By dusk, Milo and Robert had completed repairs on the barn siding. They were sitting in front of the springhouse chatting like old friends when Jenny approached. "It looks pretty good," she said, nodding in the direction of the repair.

"Pretty good?" Robert frowned, "Why, the craftsmanship is unparalleled." Milo's grin was so broad Jenny thought his face might split.

"Well, I suppose I need to have a closer look then." She turned toward the barn.

Milo leapt to his feet and caught up with her. "He said I could call him Robert." Jenny grinned and patted his shoulder.

At the barn, she pretended to engage in a critical examination of the work before calling over her shoulder so Robert could hear, "Well, it is better than average." She turned then and followed Milo back to the springhouse.

"You're a hard boss," Robert said, mischief in his eye.

"Keeps the help alert," she responded, veering off toward the house. "You two wash up for supper."

At the end of the meal, Jenny turned to Milo. "I'll need Jethro tomorrow." Milo nodded, rose and left the house.

"It's pretty dark out there," Robert said. "How far away is Jethro?"

"About three miles by road, less than a mile through the woods." She nodded toward the door. "He could make the trip blindfolded."

"Don't you worry about him? I mean with the animals out there?"

Jenny smiled. "Sure I do, but I think he probably knows every predator in the woods and has named them, and they know him. I believe he might even be the alpha male out there."

Robert cocked his head. "Why do you need Jethro?"

"If you're going to work for me you'll need suitable clothes. He'll go into Luray and buy them for you."

"Why all the way to Luray? Isn't that quite a ways off?" Jenny nodded.

"Well I guess I can be ready in the morning."

Jenny shook her head. "You need to stay here. It's better if only he goes."

Frowning, he asked, "Am I your prisoner, or something?"

"Of course not," she said. "I just don't want anyone to know you're up here, and Jethro will have to go to the bank to get money for the clothes."

"Why?"

"Because I pay cash for anything I need."

"No, I meant why don't you want anyone to know?"

Jenny chewed her lip, shook her head then answered, "I want you to trust me on this. I will tell you soon, but not yet. Will you trust me?"

Robert's eyes scanned her face. He looked out the window then back into her eyes. "Okay, but I want to know soon."

Jenny nodded. "What size shoe do you wear?"

Chapter 13

Jethro's old Scout chugged up the rutted hill shortly after sunup. Jenny gave him some banking instructions that included opening another account and depositing fifty-five dollars every week in it automatically. She introduced Robert then adjourned to her garden, leaving the two men alone to talk about the work clothes Robert would want. Twenty minutes later Jenny saw Jethro lumber back to his truck. She reached Robert just as the old man started the vehicle.

"It will take him all day to drive there, shop and drive back," Jenny said as they watched the truck rattle around the bend and out of sight.

"Why do you want me to be invisible?" he asked without turning.

"Not now."

"When?"

"Soon."

"How soon?"

Jenny put a hand on his wiry shoulder. "Soon as I'm sure," she answered and walked toward the house, leaving him in the center of the dusty yard.

Inside, Milo was sitting at the table reading a battered world history text, brow knitted in concentration. "How are you doing?"

"They's an awful lot of wars in history."

Jenny sat next to him. "Why do you think that is?" He shrugged. "Think about it. There's no right or wrong answer when you give an opinion."

"Seems like folks just ain't happy with what they got. Like they always want more."

60

"Certainly does seem that way," Jenny agreed. "I'd say you hit the nail on the head there." The boy beamed. "I think that's enough work for today," she said.

Milo slammed the book closed then realized he hadn't marked his place. He reopened it, found the page and slipped the dog-eared library bookmark into it. Rising, book in hand, he scurried up to his loft and deposited it on the small shelf by his headboard then hurried down and outside. Standing at the sink, Jenny watched him disappear into the woods, she suspected he'd head back to the reservoir.

She sat at the table resting her chin in her hands. What could she do about Milo? What if somebody saw him down there watching the nude swimmers? He was careful and adept at hiding himself, but it could happen. What then? With a deep sigh, Jenny stood and walked to the sink. The tool shed door hung open.

Robert emerged, arms loaded with an assortment of tools, which he dropped in a heap before going back inside. Jenny watched him repeat the action seven or eight times then she went outside, crossing the yard to the door where he stood. "What are you doing?"

"I figured since I'm the new handyman I ought to know what tools I have at my disposal." He spread his arms, indicating the pile.

Jenny nodded. "Now that you have them strewn all over my yard, what's next?"

"Next I organize them out here then I find or build places for them in there." He indicated the tool shed with a thumb as if he were hitchhiking.

She nodded and turned to go.

"When can I know?" he asked.

"Soon," she answered, then in a whisper, "very soon."

When she reached the porch, Jenny stopped and leaned against the corner post, her back to the tool shed. She stayed still, hearing the clank and rattle of tools being moved. When the noise stopped she turned to see Robert walking toward her. She took a deep breath and strode to meet him.

"Now," she said. "Come." She led him into the barn and across the dirt floor, stopping in front of a heavy door of rough-sawn planks. Withdrawing the peg from the hasp, Jenny threw the door open, revealing a windowless room about the size of a large closet. Most of it was taken up by a platform containing a straw mattress. At one end, attached to a sturdy iron ring in the wall, lay a pair of shackles. "This is where I slept, most of the time." Before he could speak she slammed the door and dropped the peg back in the hasp.

"Milo's father kidnapped me, eleven - almost twelve years ago. I was in a bar in Roanoke celebrating my resignation as an Air Force nurse. This big lumberjack type bought me a drink, then another." She bit her lip then continued, words coming more quickly now as if they couldn't wait to get out. "He was handsome with a nice smile and he was interested in this thirty-five-year-old ex-Air Force captain who was just passing through town. After more drinks I went outside with him. That's when he attacked. He tied and gagged me and tossed me in the back of his Jeep and brought me here." She pointed to the door, stared at the dark brown wood then put both hands against it. "He raped me, I don't know how many times, in here." She pounded the door with her open hands. "Later, he brought me a dress to wear. He took me to the springhouse and cleaned me up then told me to put it on. He threatened to kill me if I didn't behave, then he took me to the house and introduced me to Milo," she choked back a sob, "… this frightened little three-year-old, as his new mom."

Robert reached for her but she stepped away. "No, let me finish."

She walked toward the other side of the barn, to the feed bin. "The ... Milo looked so terribly frightened. I knelt in front of him and smiled and opened my arms and he just melted into them." Jenny grinned briefly through her tears then the grin became a grimace as she continued. "I was to take care of the boy ... Milo ... feed him and make sure he went to bed when he was supposed to. Carl, that was the monster's name, handled his training and discipline, and mine.

"He taught Milo about the woods, identified the plants and animals and made him memorize them to avoid a beating. I ... I always went along. He tethered me so I couldn't run; I hobbled after them." She took a shuddering breath. "Milo took to the training like he was born to it. Maybe he was, I don't know. At night, after Milo was asleep, Carl would either rape me in the bed or take me back to ..." she nodded toward the room, "then come get me in the morning." Jenny leaned against the locked feed bin, gathering her strength.

"What happened to Carl?"

She hurried outside with Robert at her heels. At the locked door to the smokehouse, she stopped and turned. "I killed him nine years ago, in there." She pointed to the door.

Eyes wide, Robert hesitated then, "Is he ... in ..."

Jenny shook her head. "No." He looked relieved. "He's ... he's not."

"Milo?"

"He doesn't remember," she answered, calming herself. "The reason I didn't want ... anyone to know about you is, nobody but Jethro knows he's dead."

"But ..."

"He was a real recluse, Carl was. He never left the hills, except when he kidnapped me that is." She let out a short laugh. "Jethro always did any shopping and everything else involving civilization, just the way he does for me."

Robert leaned against the smokehouse door. Jenny watched his face change as he tried to wrap his mind around everything she'd told him. Many minutes later he asked, "What happened to Milo's mother?"

"I don't know. He might have killed her. I just don't know."

Robert stepped forward and wrapped Jenny in his arms. She returned his embrace, resting her head on his shoulder while she allowed herself to weep. They stood rocking gently like lovers on a dance floor, for several minutes until Robert's hands drifted to her hips and she stiffened.

"No, not now." Hands on his shoulders, she freed herself and stepped away, but didn't leave. Standing instead at arm's length, she examined his face. She saw the briefest flash of anger followed by sadness and, she thought, pity. Though that raised her hackles she understood and kept herself in check. Then Robert spoke.

"Come on. Let me show you my ideas for the newly organized tool shed." Jenny followed, wiping her eyes with her forearm. Inside the shed, she let him point out all the new storage he'd build and how the tools would be arranged. She appreciated his effort to bring her out of the horrors she'd shared with him and tried, with half-smiles and nods, to show it. When he completed the tour, Jenny planted a quick kiss on his cheek and hurried out to her garden.

The morning drifted away, filled with the sharp rap of Robert's hammer from the tool shed and the soft scrape of Jenny's hoe in the soil. By the time the waning shadows signaled noon, she had pulled her mind back to the present, had shackled the pain back into its dark, locked room. She straightened and leaned the hoe against the gatepost on her way out of the garden. Sweat glued her dress to her back and she tugged it loose, feeling the coolness of the evaporating dampness under the thin fabric. She walked to the springhouse, opened the small door, drew out a large mason jar of goat's milk Jethro had brought that morning and carried it to the house.

Robert appeared at the tool shed door, shirtless torso sweat-streaked with dirt. Jenny displayed the jar and nodded toward the house. He disappeared inside the shed as she passed then she heard the door close and his steps hurrying to catch up. Inside, she pumped water into the washbasin, splashed it on her face and neck and wiped her arms. She yanked a towel off its peg, stepping aside to let Robert wash. Drying her face and arms, she watched the tight wiry muscles of his back flex when he splashed water on his torso and rubbed it with his wet hands. When he turned away from the basin she handed him the towel then stepped past him. Lifting a small cloth from a nail above the sink, Jenny soaked it in the basin, squeezed excess water out of it and began to wash his back. Robert gasped when the cool wet cloth touched him then stood still except for an occasional shiver while Jenny wiped the dirt away. She dropped the cloth on the drain board at her back then reached around him to retrieve the towel he held in both hands. At her movement he turned and looped the towel over her back, pulling her tight against him.

"Your back's wet," she whispered, tugging at the end of the towel. He let it go, sliding his hands along her sides to her hips. Breath quickening, Jenny reached around him until she had the towel in both hands. She dried his back while he traced the curve of her hips through the sweat-damp dress, until she dropped the towel and grabbed handfuls of his hair and pulled his mouth to hers.

She pushed him against the table with her body, slid her hands down his back and around to his belt. Worrying the buckle open, she pulled away long enough to wrench his pants and underwear below his knees. She pushed him onto the table, pulled her dress over her head and mounted him. Her nails dug into his shoulders, hands flexing with every push of her pelvis. He gripped her writhing hips then slid his hands up her sweat-slick back, pulling her close. Later, they lay side-by-side on the small table, exhausted.

Jenny rose and located her dress in a heap on the floor. The angle of the sun through the window told her they were at least an hour into the afternoon. She slipped the dress over her head, straightened it across her hips and tapped Robert on the shoulder. "Hungry?"

Chapter 14

Jethro arrived at dusk. Jenny and Robert met the old man in the yard. She noticed that he didn't meet Robert's eyes when they shook hands and wondered how long it would take before that changed, if it ever did. Recognizing that her thought contained the word ever, she shuddered. What was she doing?

"Thanks for your trouble, Jethro," Robert said when all the packages were unloaded. Offering his hand to the big man, he added, "Much obliged."

"Weren't nothin'," Jethro answered. He turned to go then spun around with a quickness that startled Jenny. "Uh, Mr. Robert, I'm real sorry."

"About what?"

"I'm sorry you wasn't dead."

"What?"

"I mean, I wouldn't a dumped you in them woods less'n you was, but you wasn't, so I'm sorry I done it."

Robert laughed. "It's alright Jethro, really. I'm just happy Milo found me before you got back."

The big man looked relieved. "Me too. I'da sure been sorry buryin' you when you wasn't dead, I would."

"I'm pleased to hear you say that, Jethro. Thanks again ... for everything."

Jethro nodded, accepted Jenny's hug and left.

"You just took a great burden off the old man," she said, helping Robert gather the parcels at their feet. They carried everything to the tool shed, where she noticed that he had built shelving for his personal things in addition to the work he'd done arranging the tools. "Looks nice."

"I'd rather be staying in the house."

Jenny shook her head. "Not yet, maybe not ever." She left the shed and walked toward the house.

Robert caught up with her. "Is it Milo?"

She nodded. "I have to figure out how to help him understand ... us. It wouldn't be good for him to see you there unless I can convince him."

"Don't you mean until?" he asked, frowning. "It seems pretty straightforward to me."

"I wish it was." They reached the porch and she turned toward him. "Supper in about half an hour." After a quick scan of their surroundings she kissed Robert. Breaking it off before he could react, she hurried inside.

Jenny retrieved a can of kidney beans from the pantry shelf. She stoked the stove and placed the cast iron frying pan over an open port to heat while she chopped a small onion and a pepper she'd picked the day before. She was about to toss butter into the warm pan when her ear caught a sound. "Milo?"

"Uh-huh." Came from the loft, followed by rapid breathing.

"You okay, boy?" She hurried toward the ladder.

"Uh-huh." More rapid breathing.

Jenny put one foot on the bottom rung and stopped, listening. Carefully, she raised herself on the rung and peaked over the edge of the loft. Milo lay on his back, eyes closed, masturbating. She ducked below the edge and lowered herself to the floor. Back at the stove she called, "Supper in ten minutes."

"Uh ... huh," was the breathless response.

Chapter 15

Milo was subdued during the meal. If he noticed Robert's new work clothes, he gave no indication of it. He looked mostly at his plate, sometimes at Robert, never at Jenny. When he had sopped the last of his beans up with a biscuit, he rose and mumbled "snares" on his way out the door.

"What's up with Milo?"

Jenny looked at her untouched meal then up at Robert. "He was masturbating up in his bed when I came in to make supper."

Robert's face reddened. "He was?" She nodded. He took another mouthful of food, chewed and swallowed it. "What're you going to do?"

Jenny cocked her head. "What do you mean?"

"Well, you don't want him jacking off all over the place, do you?"

Jenny frowned. "It's a natural thing for a boy to do."

"That may be, but he's got to learn to control himself." He gestured toward the window with his spoon. "Unless you want him humping everything in sight like some dog in heat."

Jenny stared at him. "He's not some kind of animal."

Robert put down his spoon and looked into her eyes and said in a soft gentle voice, "Then why do you treat him like one?"

She leaped to her feet. "where in pluperfect hell do you get off saying something like that?" she pounded her fists on the table. "Get out of here while you're still able!"

Still speaking softly, he added, "Think about it, for just a minute, please." The pained look in his eyes, stopped her from throwing her plate at him. "I didn't think much about it until you said 'alpha male' then things started to mesh in my head." He ticked points off on his fingers. "You send him out to fetch things, people. You let him wander off for days at a time without asking where he's going or where he's been. You train him with books. Half the time he's around you call him 'Boy'. You stroke his head. And in all the time I've been here I've never once heard you tell him you love him." Jenny sink back into her chair. Robert leaned forward and put his hand on hers.

She struggled to take a breath. Finally, she managed a raspy inhale and choked out, "Robert ..., leave ... leave me alone ... now."

He slid off his chair, hand still resting on hers and knelt close. "I'll be in the shed," he whispered.

Jenny sat unmoving; the echo of the terrible indictment rang in her ears. She hated him, loved him, and feared he was right.

Chapter 16

"Maw? You okay, Maw?" Jenny felt Milo's hand on her shoulder and slowly realized she'd fallen asleep sitting at the table. She sat up, flexing out the stiffness in her shoulders.

"I'm fine, Milo." She smiled at him. "I must have dozed."

"It's near dawn, Maw."

Startled, Jenny glanced at the window and saw the graying sky. She stood. "Did you just come home?" He nodded. "Where were you?" He shrugged. She looked him over carefully, saw that his thick hair was damp and felt fear pushing her toward panic. She pushed back, took a breath. "Were you at the reservoir?" Milo looked at his feet. "Tell, boy." He shook his head. "I mean it, Milo." She raised her voice a notch. "Tell me, now," she commanded.

His head jerked up and he stared, eyes wide. Jenny saw his Adams Apple working as he tried to swallow. "I wus."

"Tell!"

He took a step back then another until he was leaning against the bedpost. "I wus up the sycamore, watchin'. I think they wus the same ones as last time. They wus passin' round a jug like Paw useta get 'n made him so mean, only they was laughin' 'n such, not hittin'." He stopped and inspected his feet.

"More!"

He shrugged then continued. "I watched a long time 'n they begun fallin' down 'n laughin'. One a the girls took off all 'er clothes 'n flopped in the water 'n the rest done the same ... boys too. 'ventually they all clumb out 'n got dry by the fire. Some put clothes on 'n some not.

They did some more jug passin', but not so much, 'n soon they was all asleep, like Paw." He stopped, his eyes darting side to side, avoiding Jenny's.

"Milo!"

"When I was sure, I clumb down 'n swum across." He slid into a crouch, arms hugging his knees. "Maw, them girls is so purty." Jenny clamped her jaws tight, felt her pulse throbbing and nodded for him to continue. "I … I swum across 'n snuck up to … to the girl … the one who got nekkid fust. She was breathin' slow 'n the sleepin' bag was slidin' off her … breasts." He took a long breath, hugged his knees tighter and rested his chin on them. His gaze was far away from the cabin. "I slunk up close 'n touched one real careful. I was ready to scoot, I was, but she kep' sleepin' so … so, I touched t'other one 'n rubbed it some." His breath quickened. "She smiled, Maw, but she didn't rouse. She moaned, too. I rubbed s'more 'n she kep' smilin' 'n moanin' 'n it felt real fine." He smiled, looked at Jenny and lost the smile. "Then … then she rolled away from me, on her side, 'n the cover slid down futher. Maw, I wanted to touch more, but I got afeared she'd rouse so I just lay away off 'n looked some more. I stayed till someone stirred across the fire. Then I swum back 'n come home."

Jenny fought the rage and fear building inside her. "Stand up!" She closed the gap between them in two steps and slapped him hard. Despite being her height and probably outweighing her by a few pounds, Milo cowered against the bedpost. She reached for him, grabbing both shoulders and held him straight. "Listen to me! You must never, never touch a girl without her permission. Do you hear me?" She shook him. He nodded, eyes indicating he was on the edge of panic. "What you did was terrible. It was wrong." She took a calming breath and continued. "I don't want you to go back there. Do you hear?" He nodded. Jenny let him go then and he scooted up the ladder into his loft. She could hear him whimpering as she hurried outside.

On the porch, she collapsed against the corner post and slid to the floor. The sun was just peaking over the ridge. She looked at the yard, the barn, her garden, the tool shed, and took several ragged breaths. Hands covering her eyes, she sobbed.

Before she felt ready, she forced herself to stop crying, rose and steadied herself, and left the porch. She strode toward the open barn door, breath coming in gasps. She crossed the threshold without slowing, seeing the door to her prison grow larger with each step as if meeting her half way. She pulled the peg, opened the door and stepped inside. She sat on the straw mattress, back to the wall, hugging her knees and watched the heavy door swing shut. In the darkness, the familiar darkness, she worked through the mantras that had kept her sane in her prison, calming breath after calming breath, until she felt her mind begin to focus. As her eyes adjusted to the absence of light, familiar gray lines, the tiny spaces between the boards, formed four columns in the opposite wall. Jenny used the columns to sort her thoughts, to categorize her options, to form her conclusions. She saw the words as clearly as if they'd been written in chalk on a board.

By the time Jenny left the barn, the sun showed mid-morning. Rounding the corner of the cabin, she saw Robert and Milo sitting on the porch.

"Where have you been?" Robert asked. "We were worried." Milo stared at his feet.

"I went for a walk," she answered. "Have you two eaten?"

"I fried some eggs. Want me to make you some?" Jenny shook her head and walked past them into the house. Milo continued scrutinizing his toes.

Inside, she went to the sink, pumped the washbasin full, and splashed water on her face. She saw Robert and Milo walk toward the tool shed, with the man making drawing motions in the air and pointing toward the springhouse and the boy nodding. When they disappeared into the shed, Jenny pulled off her dress, dropping it in a pile of laundry near the door and walked over to the big footlocker in the corner. She opened it, retrieved a similar shift dress and put it on the table. She washed at the sink then turned and reached for the dress then stopped, remembering, reliving how less than twenty-four hours ago she had tried, on that table, to devour Robert with her body. She slipped the clean dress over her head then gathered the laundry and went outside.

Robert and Milo were across the yard, setting up a pair of sawhorses. Robert glanced in her direction, said something to Milo then hurried to the tool shed emerging with a small armload of clothes. He met Jenny at the washstand and added them to the rumpled heap on the rough bench. He moved close enough to touch her hip, blocking Milo's view with his body.

"Don't," she whispered.

"He can't see."

She pulled his hand away and squeezed it gently. "Don't count on it."

Robert walked back to the work area he and Milo were setting up and Jenny went back to her laundry.

By noon, she'd washed, wrung, and hung the clothes and had lunch going. Watching the approach of man and boy through the window over the sink, she went back over her decision, looking for holes, looking for better alternatives, but once again concluded that it was what she had to do.

By the time the two entered, Jenny had the washbasin filled and towels ready. They cleaned up and

74

took their places for the meal. She set plates of stew at each place then went back to the stove to retrieve the biscuits. Turning toward the table, she saw Milo sliding his spoon around the plate, pushing the food into piles, not eating. She put the bowl of biscuits in the middle of the table then stepped behind Milo and crouched close to his ear, both hands on his shoulders. "It's alright, Milo," she whispered and kissed his cheek. When she sat and looked up, he was staring at her, eyes questioning, unsure. She nodded and smiled. Finally, he ate.

When his plate lay empty, wiped clean by his third biscuit, Milo rose and looked at Robert.

"I'll be out in a bit, Milo." The boy nodded and left. "He's been acting strange all day. What's up?"

Jenny didn't answer. When Robert started to stand, she put her hand over his. "Sit a minute."

"What's up?" He sat, leaning forward.

She examined his face and saw real concern in his eyes. "What do you know about cars?"

He straightened. "Not the fucking car thing again. I thought we were through with that." He yanked his hand free and headed for the door.

Jenny leapt up and caught his arm. "No it's not that. I need to know if you know anything about cars."

"I know they have four wheels and an engine."

"Shit," she spat. "So you don't know anything about making them run." She scooped plates from the table and hauled them to the sink.

"I didn't say that." He approached the sink and put a hand on her shoulder.

"Well, do you?"

"I grew up on a farm. You learn a little about a lot of things."

"Did you learn about cars?"

"Some."

"Dammit! Can you fix a car or not!"

"Easy, easy. That's not a simple question. Besides, why is that even a question? I haven't seen anything with an engine since I woke up here, except Jethro's heap." Jenny grabbed his arm and led him out the door. When she let go and hurried toward the work area and Milo, he followed. Milo looked up and smiled at their approach.

"Maw. Look the way we got all them tools lined up, ready. We gonna make a washin' place here fer the game after skinnin'." He pointed to the outside wall of the smokehouse.

"That'll be good, Milo." She smiled at him. "Right now I need you to check your snares to see if we have a rabbit for dinner.

He frowned. "I checked this mornin'. It's a bit early."

"There might be something. Check them for me, please." Milo nodded and loped toward the treeline.

Robert grabbed Jenny's arm as she turned away. "What the hell's going on?" He spun her around to face him.

"You'll see," she said, pulling away. She stepped inside the tool shed. Returning with a large pry bar, she hurried toward the rutted road. Robert rushed to catch up. At the point the road sloped downward, Jenny turned hard left so quickly that he skidded on the dirt trying to change direction. She led the way through low brush that had pretty much devoured an old carriage road. In a few more strides, a long, low tin-roofed building became visible, it's big double doors secured with a rusted hasp and lock. Jenny hooked the pry bar under the hasp and yanked. On the second pull, the wood holding the staple split and the hasp fell open. Jenny tossed the bar aside barely missing Robert, and pulled on the door.

"Help me," she said. Robert stepped up beside her and grabbed the side of the door. It took several minutes before they were able to wrestle both doors partially open. Inside, sat two tarp-covered vehicles, one behind the other. Jenny yanked the tarp off the first, an olive-drab Jeep; without hesitating she went to the second and revealed a dark red Buick sedan.

"Holy shit! What … who's …?" Robert stammered.

"The Buick's mine," she said. "After Carl brought me here and locked me up, he went through my purse and got the keys." She shook her head. "He must have seen me in the parking lot because he knew what car I drove." She turned toward Robert, who stood mouth open looking from one car to the other. "He went back and got the car and brought it here. I'm guessing with Jethro. After I'd been imprisoned maybe a week, he brought me here to show me." Her mouth contorted. "He said, 'Won't nobody be lookin' for you bitch.' I had actually thought someone would notice the car abandoned and start a search … or something." She shook her head. "'Won't nobody be lookin' for you bitch,' he said. Then good old Carl the bastard Larson bent me over the hood of my own car and sodomized me."

Robert put his arms around her and held tight, expecting her tears, but they didn't come. Jenny freed herself. "Can you get either one running?"

"I don't know. Why do you want them, anyway? You worried old Jethro's going to kick off, or something? I mean you don't ever leave; you don't want me to leave;

I've got no idea what you have planned for Milo. What's up?"

"I'll tell you soon," she said.

He frowned and shook his head. "No. If I'm going to bust my butt trying to get one of these running I want to know why."

Jenny paced back and forth between the two machines, finally stopping in front of Robert. "We're going to leave. We have to."

Robert's brow furrowed. "Why all of a sudden?"

Jenny walked past him and out the door without answering. When he caught up and touched her arm she stopped, facing him. "I need to take Milo somewhere safe, away from here."

"What's happened?"

"Nothing ... yet." She resumed her pace, Robert by her side.

"I'm having a bit of trouble here," he said. "If nothing's changed, why the need to leave?"

"Things are changing, Milo's changing."

"How?"

Jenny shook her head and walked faster. When they reached the workstation beside the smokehouse, she turned and grabbed Robert by the shoulders. "Just get something running, please."

He must have seen in her face, the fear that fought to control her. He placed his hands over hers, squeezing gently. "Okay, I'll try." He frowned then. "How do we keep Milo from finding out?"

Her face clouded. "We don't. I'll tell him something ... I'll tell him we're going to visit one of your relatives. Do you have any relatives?"

"No, I told you. Why not one of yours?"

Jenny looked away. "I ... don't have any."

Robert cocked his head, eyes questioning then said, "Alright, I have an old friend, you might say a pseudo-sister, in Minnesota." He turned and started back toward the hidden garage then stopped. "I don't guess you know where any car keys are, do you?" She shook her head. He nodded and continued down the road.

Jenny reached the porch just as Milo emerged from the tree line. He held a dead rabbit high for her to see. "You was right, Maw." She nodded and went inside. Several minutes later, Milo entered with the skinned and eviscerated carcass in hand and plopped it on the table across from where Jenny sat quartering newly washed potatoes. He went to the sink and rinsed the blood from his hands, drying them on his pant legs then turned. "Where's Robert? He wadn't up by the smokehouse."

She put down her knife and motioned for Milo to take a seat. Looking troubled, he obeyed. "He's doing another job for us right now."

Puzzled, Milo asked, "Where? He wadn't anywhere in sight."

"You remember the garage in the woods?"

Milo's eyes widened. "Paw's place? But, we ..." Jenny raised a hand and he clamped his jaws shut.

"I know what we said, Milo. We weren't ever going in there, but Robert has to go somewhere. He needs to visit his sister."

"Why ain't Jethro jus' takin' him to town?"

"Because you and I are going with him."

Milo's expression changed as he processed the information.

"When we goin'?"

"It depends on what he can do with the cars."

The boy nodded then frowned, looking troubled. "We gonna finish the washin' place fust?"

Jenny shook her head. Her teeth worried her lower lip for a second then she answered. "It will have to wait until we get back." Watching Milo's face, she knew he didn't believe her. He hesitated then nodded, rose and went outside.

Jenny carried the stewpot containing the potatoes and other chopped vegetables to the sink, pumped it half full of water and put it over an open port on the stove. After boning and cubing the headless carcass, she added it to the pot then secured the lid and tossed two more splits into the firebox. Outside she saw Milo at the newly assembled workstation looking lost and felt a tear run down her cheek. "So much is going to change for you," she said, shaking her head as she rinsed the knife. When she looked out the window again Milo was gone.

Panic knotted her chest. She rushed to the door, outside and across the yard, scanning the tree line in a futile gesture. At the crest of the hill that was the terminus of the rutted road, she caught a glimpse of the boy as he disappeared in the direction of the garage. Jenny heaved a long sigh. "Calm down girl," she mumbled and turned away from the hill.

She crossed the yard to the clothesline to retrieve the dry clothes. Sorting them on the washstand, she ran through the details of her plan again. The key was the vehicle, whichever one worked. She'd get Jethro to close the accounts and bring the money up. She'd sign the cars over to him and have him register the one they'd be taking. They'd pack up and head west, somewhere; the 'where' she'd figure out on the way. She knew she had to keep Milo thinking they'd return for as long as she could.

Jenny dropped Robert's laundry off at the tool shed then took the rest into the house. She was putting her clothes in the footlocker when Robert came in. She closed it quickly and met him at the table.

"The keys were in the cars, still in the ignition," he said, shaking his head. "Both batteries are dead as doornails and the tires on the Buick are all flat. The Jeep is on blocks so the tires are in better shape but I don't know about the rest." He walked to the sink and filled the washbasin then began scrubbing the grime from his hands and arms before continuing. "Rats or something ate into the ignition wires and hoses, maybe some of the rest of the wiring too. I won't know until we get a battery in it." He dried his hands and arms.

Jenny nodded and turned toward the stove to tend the bubbling stewpot. "Did you send Milo to Jethro's?" she asked.

"No, but I will. Where is he?" She froze. "What's wrong, Jenny?"

Her voice cracked. "He wasn't with you in the garage?"

"I haven't seen him since you sent him out looking for rabbits."

She closed her eyes tight, placing both hands flat on the table to keep from falling.

"Jenny?" Robert stepped to her side. "Jen? What's wrong?"

Straightening quickly, she shoved him aside and raced out the door and into the woods, stumbling over exposed roots in her haste. She heard him behind her but ignored his calls and kept running. A few hundred yards along the path she tripped and sprawled face down in dust and lay there weeping.

81

Robert reached her and dropped to his knees. "Are you hurt?" He pulled her close.

"Milo," she said through tears.

"What about him?"

She dug her fingers into his back. "He's gone."

"What do you mean, gone? He goes out all the time."

"No, he's gone. I know it."

"How can you know?"

"I told him … I told him we were going to … to visit your sister." She stopped to catch her breath through her sobs. "He wanted to know if we were ever coming back and I told him we were. I could see in his face. He knew I was lying. I never … never lied to him like that." Jenny pushed out of Robert's embrace and rose. She stood gazing into the thick forest, her breath coming in short gasps until she drew a deep gulp of air into her lungs and let out a long sigh.

Pivoting on her heel, she almost tripped over the still-kneeling Robert. He stood. "What now?" he asked, holding her.

Jenny pried his hands from her waist. "We find him." She slipped past him, striding back toward the cabin.

Inside, Jenny stirred the stew, put the heavy iron cover on the pot and stoked the fire. She sat then, elbows resting on the table, chin in her hands, eyes closed. Robert sat silently across the table.

Finally he asked, "Do you have any idea where he might have gone?"

Jenny opened her eyes and sat up straight. She took a couple of long breaths and answered, "I think he'll be around the reservoir somewhere. He's been really interested in the young people swimming there, especially the girls." She nodded, agreeing with herself. "In the morning I'll go down there and take a look."

"I'll go with you."

"No. I still want you to fix that damn Jeep. I'll stop by Jethro's and have him bring a battery up."

Robert started to protest but stopped when she hardened her stare. "Okay," he said. "Have him get ignition wires also. Does he know what year the Jeep is?"

Jenny frowned. "I'm sure he does." She rose, grabbed a towel and lifted the lid on the pot. She stirred it twice then scooped a bit onto the wooden spoon, blew on it and sipped. "This is ready," she announced.

Robert got two bowls from the shelf, handing each to her in turn. He placed them on the table when she handed them back then grabbed two spoons off the drain board, placing one by each bowl.

They ate silently, neither looking at the other. Robert took a second helping and was almost finished with it before Jenny had emptied her plate for the first time. "Good," he said after the last spoonful disappeared into his mouth.

Jenny nodded and stood, reaching for his bowl. She padded to the sink, rinsed both bowls in cold water and soap and propped them on the drain. Ignoring Robert, she strode to her bed, pulled her dress over her head and climbed under the cover, her back to the room.

She heard the chair scrape as Robert rose, listened to him breath and finally followed the sound of his steps to the door and beyond.

Chapter 17

Jenny woke to the drumming of rain on the cabin's tin roof. She slipped out of bed and picked her dress off its hook on the wall and put it on. Stepping onto the bed rail she peaked into Milo's loft, hoping he would be there, knowing he wouldn't. She teased the fire in the stove awake and set the half-full coffee pot on it to reheat yesterday's brew then looked out the window to see if there was any activity at the tool shed. Seeing none, she fried two eggs and slid them onto a plate then sliced a thick chunk from the two-day-old sourdough loaf and sat at the table. She was finishing a cup of the bitter coffee when Robert came in, rain-soaked shirt clinging to his thin frame.

"Damn, it's wet out there." Jenny nodded and rose. Grabbing a dry towel from the shelf above the sink, she tossed it to him then retrieved two more eggs from the basket, dropped a lump of butter into the warm cast-iron pan and watched it melt before breaking the eggs into it.

"Coffee's old." She nodded toward the pot. Robert retrieved a cup and poured the dark liquid into it then sat at the table. Jenny served his breakfast then poured another cup and sat.

"How far away is this reservoir?"

"Four or five miles."

Robert shook his head. "Are you seriously going to go in this weather?"

Jenny nodded and finished her coffee in one long swallow. She rose and went to the large footlocker and opened it. Kneeling, she lifted the shallow tray containing her current meager wardrobe and placed it on the floor. She pushed aside the tightly rolled uniforms until she located her rain slicker. Setting it on the bed, she returned the tray and closed the lid. She shook open the rain gear and slipped it over her head. When she reached the door she stopped and glanced at Robert. "Please go to the Jeep and try to figure out what else you might need so you can tell Jethro when he comes." She stepped outside and hurried into the forest.

It took her thirty-five minutes to make the trip down to Jethro's small farm. When she broke though the tree line into the cleared area near his barn a huge golden mongrel came charging across the yard toward her. Jenny fought the urge to run and tried to remember what Milo had told her about this monster.

It was twenty feet away when Jethro appeared at the barn door, surprised when he recognized her. "Rocky! No!" The beast skidded to a stop, turned and trotted toward his master. "Git on back!" Jethro ordered, pointing at the clapboard house with the large wrench he held. The dog's head and tail lowered, he veered off his path to follow the order.

"Miss Jenny?" Jethro lumbered into the yard. "Ain't never seen you here."

"I need you to bring some things up the hill," she said.

"How come you didn't send Milo?" He stopped a few feet away looking puzzled, rain dripping from the bill of his greasy cap. The wrench hung at his side, the handle lost in his huge fist.

"No time now, Jethro. Here's what I need." She went through the details slowly, making sure he understood about the vehicles and the money. When she finished, she had him repeat the instructions. Satisfied, she turned to leave.

"Miss Jenny?" When she turned back to face him, he asked, "How come Milo didn't come?"

85

She wanted to get on with the search without worrying the big man about his young friend. "He's out in the woods somewhere and I couldn't wait for him. I've got to get along now, Jethro." He nodded but didn't move; his brow creased. Jenny left him standing in the rain. Glancing back once she reentered the woods, she saw he hadn't moved and it worried her a little. She shook off the feeling and continued along the narrow game trail until it forked. She took the left fork, resuming her descent toward the large artificial lake in the valley to the east. As she walked, she looked for signs of Milo's passage, cursing the rain for obliterating the remote possibility that she'd see any.

Jenny became aware that the rain had stopped. Rays of the emerging sun knifed through the trees and lit the forest floor in a diamond-like mist. She flipped the hood of the poncho off and ran her fingers through her sweat-matted hair and stopped for a moment to get her bearings. By the glint of sun through the clouds she judged the time to be a little after noon, which meant she'd been away from the cabin more than four hours. She considered turning back on the chance that Milo had returned but rejected the idea with a shake of her head. As she was about to take her next step, she heard a twig snap and spun in the direction of the sound to see Jethro a few feet away, his brow furrowed.

He closed the gap between them with remarkable speed and threw a flour sack over her head, holding it tight against Jenny's struggles.

"Jethro? What ... ?"

"Mister Robert don't want to leave the mountain, Miss Jenny." He tipped her head back and the sack suddenly was damp around her mouth and nose. "I'm real sorry," were the last words she heard before the sweet smelling chloroform took over.

Milo's Gift

Chapter 18

Jenny regained consciousness slowly. When her vision cleared she recognized the all too familiar pattern of light coming through cracks in the wooden wall and screamed "Nooooo!" until her voice cracked. Gasping for breath, she sat up on the cot and slid back into the corner, pulling her knees to her chest. She fought hard against the terrifying feeling that she'd been dreaming, that there was no Robert, that Carl was still alive, that the years without him never happened. She bit her lip against the scream that tried to force its way out of her dry throat. Her hands clawed the soiled blanket up and around her shivering body while her mind tried to make sense of … of anything. She worked back through the day as she remembered, or dreamt, it. The rain, Robert and the cars, going to Jethro's with instructions for their move, searching for Milo, Jethro coming at her, apologizing – *Sorry Miss Jenny.* Wait! He said *Mister Robert* didn't want to leave the mountain, not *Mister Carl.* Robert? She shook her head. Robert?

Jenny heard muffled voices, leapt toward the door and tried hard to make out the words but couldn't. Just as she was about to bang on the door, doubt overtook her again; she couldn't be sure, and if Carl was out there he'd punish her for the noise. She slipped back onto the cot and into her corner. Wrapping the blanket around her, she waited.

Several minutes passed and she fought drowsiness. A shadow under the door caught her attention. She tensed, pulling the blanket tighter.

"Jenny?" The door opened a crack. "Jenny, it's me Robert." He flung it wide and stepped in.

Jenny hugged the shadows. "Robert?" The relief she felt quickly turned to confusion. "Why did …?"

"Jenny, I'm so sorry," Robert said, rushing to sit on the cot beside her. "Jethro must have misunderstood what I meant when I said I didn't want to leave the mountain." He reached for her, pulling her to him. "I never meant for him to ... ."

She slowly relaxed into his arms, relieved, her breathing quiet and her mind working. Robert stroked her hair and back, cooing reassuring nothings. Weariness pushed at her and she drifted off for a second or two while Robert droned on until one phrase snapped her awake and she pulled away from him. "What did you say?"

"What?"

"You were saying something about Jethro."

Robert frowned. "I said that he's not too bright."

"That's not what you said."

"Okay ... okay. I said he's not much smarter than that huge cur of his, Rocky." He shrugged. "Same thing."

Jenny leapt off the cot and ran out the door. Robert followed her, shouting. He caught her at the porch and grabbed her arm. Spinning on her heel, Jenny smacked him hard, causing him to stumble backward. He straightened, holding his cheek. "Was that just because I called him stupid?" He stepped forward and Jenny swung again. This time he grabbed her wrist, ducked the roundhouse from her other hand and stepped behind her pinning her arms to her sides. "What in hell is wrong?"

"Let me go!"

"Not while you're trying to beat the crap out of me. What's your problem?"

"You're lying to me again." Jenny stopped struggling. "Now, let me go!"

"Okay, but you take another swing at me and I'll knock you on your ass." He released his grip and stepped

89

back as she spun to face him, fists clenched at her sides. "Remember what I said."

She strode past him and sat on the porch, legs pulled up to her chest. He stood a yard away facing her. "When did you visit Jethro?" she asked, watching Robert's face. What she saw was confusion.

"I'm not sure what you mean?"

"It's a pretty simple question, Robert." Jenny glared at him. "When were you down at Jethro's farm?"

He shook his head. "Never."

"Bullshit!" Jenny hopped off the porch and Robert took a step back, hands set to fend off any attack.

"I swear, Jenny. I've never seen the place."

She folded her arms across her chest. "Then how do you know Rocky?"

His confused expression morphed into a small grin. "Jethro brought him up on the truck when he came to ask about parts for the cars."

Jenny didn't believe it for a minute but decided to accept his explanation while she tried to sort out what was really going on. She nodded, turned and climbed the porch step. Stopping at the door, she spun back to face Robert. "What about the cars?"

"I'll know better when Jethro gets here with the parts I asked for," he answered.

Nodding, Jenny left him standing in the yard. At the sink, she pumped some water into the kettle then put it on the stove. She opened the firebox, teased a few small embers from the ashes, tossed a handful of dried birch bark on them then blew gently until they caught. Adding wood in ever-larger pieces, she coaxed the fire awake then closed the cast iron door.

Milo's Gift

Milo's Gift

Part II
The Tracker

Chapter 1

Marissa Landry merged onto I-95 south from the Quantico entrance ramp. She set the cruise control on the Dodge van to seventy-five and settled in for the drive to Richmond. She felt some trepidation at finally returning to the office where she was recruited a dozen years ago. Her hand went to her throat, fingers tracing the scar, triggering memories of her long hospital stay, of the three lost years in her memory. The flash of brake lights from the semi ahead brought her sharply back to the present. She slowed, checked the left lane and swerved around the truck. When she was back in her lane, having harshely admonished herself for her inattention during the pass, she devoted her attention to the drive.

A pair of young agents waited for her at the parking garage under the Richmond field office. They indicated a reserved slot near the elevator and watched her back the van into it. Marissa followed them to the elevator. The man pushed the call button, the doors slid open, both agents stepped aside to let her enter. When the elevator doors closed, the female agent spoke. "Special Agent Landry, I'm Special Agent Caroline Sharp. This is Special Agent Art Carson." Once she'd completed the introductions, Agent Sharp turned back to face the door. The two glanced at each other several times during the ride to the sixth floor. Marissa filed that information with the other random data her eyes and ears had recorded about them: their youth, absence of rings, athleticism, good looks, and minute details that she could retrieve at will to form a more complete description of them than they probably could of themselves or each other. The door slid open at six and the three stepped into a wide, brightly lit hallway.

"Missy Mae!" Harvey Delancey's bellow rattled the walls. "How you doing girl?" She turned to see his wheelchair barreling toward her. Smiling, she held her ground. The chair stopped inches from her ankles.

Marissa contained her desire to jump into his lap and hug him . "A little decorum, Harvey. You are, after all, a field office director."

"It ain't in me, girl," he laughed. "It's been a while."

"So you folks have lost somebody, Harvey." She immediately regretted the statement. Turning to look into the embarrassed faces of agents Carson and Sharp, she added, "Hey, it happens to all of us at one time or another. This old fart probably lost a bunch in his time." She nodded back to her mentor.

"I have," he agreed. "That's why I started the Tracker program. Sharp and Carson will brief you. Come by and see me when you're done." Without waiting for an answer, he spun around and scooted back to his office.

Marissa nodded to agents Carson and Sharp waiting a few yards down the hall. They turned and led her into the briefing room. Inside, large screens displayed data about the escapee. She scanned them then sat waiting for either of the agents to speak. They took seats facing her, each moved the chair a little apart from the other before settling in. "Okay," she prodded, "tell me how it happened." Carson and Sharp looked at each other then at Marissa. Carson spoke.

"We were taking him to a safe house outside Roanoke. We pulled into the driveway, got out and were approaching the front door when we heard screams coming from the tree line twenty yards west of our location. Agent Sharp responded immediately while I secured the subject to the porch railing. I joined my partner and we located the source of the screams." He shook his head.

Agent Sharp took up the narrative. "It was a teenage girl. She was standing on the path yelling her head off and pointing at a big old black snake sunning itself a few feet in front of her. I picked the thing up and moved it over to a large rock well off the trail. We walked her past the rock and she finally calmed down." Sharp took a breath, closed her eyes and added, "When we returned to the porch he was gone. The empty cuffs were hanging from the rail." She opened her eyes and glanced at her partner. "One of us should have stayed with him."

Carson frowned. "I had to make a decision: back up my partner going into an unknown situation, or babysit a handcuffed informant."

"I had it under control," Sharp said with more than a hint of irritation.

"Had what under control?" he shot back. "You had no fucking idea what was around that corner."

"Okay," Marissa interrupted. "Knock it off! You two can argue about it over Guinness at Mackey's but not now." She pointed at Carson. "What happened next?"

"Sorry," he said. Leaning forward in his chair, he continued. "We called it in and started to scour the area. There are a lot of woods around the place and it was the first time we'd been there, so..."

Marissa cut him off. "Did you call in the locals?"

"We notified the field office," Carson answered.

Marissa shook her head. "Not what I asked. Do you want me to repeat the question?"

Agent Sharp took over. "We did not, Agent Landry. We thought we could handle it."

"Apparently you were wrong. What happened next?"

Both agents reddened. Sharp took a breath.

"We searched for over an hour," Carson offered. "Concentric circles moving outward, standard procedure, you know the drill; we knew we were running out of time." He shrugged.

Marissa looked from one to the other. "Did you have the area cordoned off before you obscured his trail?" She had thought about leaving out the accusation but wanted them not to make the same mistakes again. Sharp reddened; Carson frowned. Both shook their heads.

"What about the screamer?"

"She ... was gone from the area." Sharp answered, head down. "I didn't occur to ...us that she might have been a diversion." She glanced at her partner, who nodded agreement. "Nobody knew we were taking him to the safe house."

"Okay, thanks." Neither one moved. "We're done here, agents. Unless you have something else?"

They looked at each other then at Marissa. Agent Carson spoke. "What are you going to do?"

"Find him," she answered. "But, I imagine that's not the question you want answered. Look, you two. You made a mistake by underestimating your subject. It's not the last mistake you'll ever make, believe me. But I trust it's one you won't make again. Shake it off and get on with your work." Marissa motioned to the door. "Now, go. I have work to do." The two agents hurried out the door, closing it gently after them.

"Now, Mr. Lars Gunderson," she whispered, gazing at the full-face image on the center screen. "Where might you be?"

Chapter 2

"Day's almost over old man," Marissa said, peaking around Harvey Delancey's open door. "How about I buy us both dinner and a good bottle of wine?"

"You talked me into it. Let me finish up the last paragraph of this report and I'm all yours."

Marissa slouched in the side chair and waited, browsing the various bulletins and charts tacked on his walls without really absorbing the contents. The fingertips of her right hand traced the long thin scar under her chin over and over again.

With a flourish, Harvey tacked a period onto the end of the final paragraph and spun his chair to face her. His eyes clouded when he noticed the position of her hand, but he masked it with a smile. "Okay, Tracker, you have my full attention."

Marissa shook her head as if to clear it. "Sorry, I zoned out for a bit there." She sat straight in the chair. "Where would you like to go?"

"What're you in the mood for?"

"I don't know, Harv. You pick."

"Okay then, the Italian place down the block."

"I'm not in the mood for Italian. How about Thai food?"

Harvey laughed. "You haven't changed, hon. Thai it is."

They went to a Thai place that Harvey said they used to frequent when she was in therapy. Marissa nodded and smiled, but when they entered the restaurant it didn't look familiar. "Are you sure we ate here?" she asked when the hostess showed them to their table.

Harvey's smile faded for a second. "Maybe not. I guess I'm getting old." He opened his menu. "Let's see whether it's worth coming back to."

Chapter 3

Shortly before dawn, Marissa woke, stretched, yawned, and cursed Doctor Harvey Delancey under her breath for insisting on the second bottle of wine. She slid out of bed and shuffled into the bathroom, silently thanking the agency for stocking their transient quarters with Advil. She took two then brushed her teeth and pulled the oversized 'Bama sweatshirt over her head, tossing it out the bathroom door. The shower almost completed her recovery but the strangeness, the feeling that there was something just outside her consciousness that wanted to come in, nagged at her. Marissa toweled off and returned to the bedroom to begin her yoga routine. Following a series of sun salutations, she assumed a full lotus position in the middle of the room, letting her mind tune to the low "a-u-m" that began deep inside her like the warning growl of a lioness.

Thirty minutes later, she rose and padded over to her duffle. Marissa tossed it on the bed, retrieved underwear, lightweight socks and a khaki jumpsuit and dressed while she formulated a search plan. By the time she'd laced up her Gortex hiking boots, she had decided to find out if there was any way the screaming young girl and the escapee were connected. Carson and Sharp would get that assignment while she returned to the site to see if she could find any trace of Gunderson the two had missed.

At 0730 Marissa entered the elevator for the trip down to the offices. Several agents who were waiting when the elevator stopped at the third floor went silent as soon as they saw her. They knew her presence meant that someone in their place had screwed up, and she guessed they already knew who it was. She felt sorry for Carson and Sharp.

101

Both agents were in the briefing room when she entered. Marissa nodded a hello and took her seat facing them. "Did either of you get the name of your screamer?"

Agent Sharp nodded. "Artie did, after we got her calmed down."

"Good. See if she has any connection to Gunderson."

"We're on it already," agent Carson said. "So far we haven't found anything but we have a couple more avenues to explore."

Marissa nodded. "Okay then. Keep me posted." She left the room and headed for the elevator. On the way, she detoured into Harvey's office. It was empty. She left a note on his keyboard briefing him on her plan then took the elevator to the parking garage. A few minutes later she was on the highway to Roanoke.

She stayed with secondary roads, passing through Appomattox then angling south of Lynchburg, past Rustburg (she laughed out loud at the name) and on through Roanoke and west to the isolated safe house near Catawba. She identified herself to the bored guards, eased up the circular drive and parked in front of the place. Around the side of the house Marissa noted the yellow crime-scene tape threaded through trees deep into the woods. "Wasted a mile of tape, looks like," she said, shaking her head.

Carson and Sharp reported that they'd marked the point where Gunderson had entered the tree line. Marissa spied the small yellow cone seventy feet away to her right and strode toward it, scanning the ground on the way. At the cone, a clear footprint told her they were right. The other prints, male and female, all around it told her it didn't matter. If they were as sloppy in the woods as they were here, any clear trail would be obliterated. "Be nice,

Marissa," she mumbled. "Consider it a challenge." She returned to the van, slid the side door wide and stepped in.

Stuffing the cargo pockets of her jumpsuit with survival gear, she laughed at herself. Even though she was going on a brief search, she felt better when completely outfitted for an extended trek. Finally, she strapped on her utility belt and holstered the tiny stun-gun at the small of her back.

Marissa stepped over the cone and walked straight into the woods. She figured Gunderson, not knowing the area, would head for the deepest cover he could find then stop to sort things out, so she did the same. She tried to get into his head, look with his eyes rather than her own for a place to hide. Within a half-mile she saw a dense stand of young pine, heavy with undergrowth and turned toward it. She scanned the bordering growth as she approached. Veering left to where some twigs were broken, she stopped and sat on her heels, arms around her knees, chin on her arms. Here was a clear point of entry. She absorbed every detail, squatting silent and still for several minutes, looking, listening. "Okay, down the rabbit hole." She said as she stood and walked into the underbrush at Gunderson's point of entry.

Thirty or so feet farther, Marissa emerged in a clearing ringed by mature trees and carpeted by a thick brown bed of pine needles. Ignoring the four spots where deer had bedded down a few days earlier, she closed in on the disturbed area near the center of the clearing and squatted again. He'd spent some time here; *Probably listening to Carson and Sharp thrash around,* she thought. She wet her nose with a little saliva then inhaled deeply several times, each time in a different direction, then stood and walked to a large tree. She nodded, *Long enough to use the little boy's tree.* A quick glance told her where he'd left his sanctuary. She followed.

Within minutes Marissa was beyond the cordoned area, moving with an easy loping stride she could keep up all day. His trail, as clear to her as a road map, led to a relatively busy secondary road two miles away from the house. Another hundred yards along the road, the trail ended with evidence that a large truck had stopped to pick him up. She photographed the depression left by the tire, and the footprint near it. Marissa returned to the van and stowed her gear then sent the photos to the lab for identification. On her way out of the driveway she told the guards to remove the tape and go home.

After dinner at a hole-in-the-wall bistro near the edge of Roanoke, Marissa settled into a room at the local Hampton Inn. A quick shower, then she spread Gunderson's file on the king-sized bed and perused the information.

Chapter 4

The next morning she called in and requested a search for trucking outfits that used that route on the off chance that they'd locate the truck that picked him up. Marissa spent a few minutes on the phone with Carson, who told her they'd reached a dead end trying to connect the screaming girl to Gunderson. Marissa had figured that the girl was coincidental so it didn't surprise her. Before signing off she said, "According to his sheet, he taught at a junior college up in West Virginia for a time. Maybe he's made contact with someone up there. He'll be needing things, clothes, money, transportation. Dig into his background and see if you come up with anyone." She flipped open the folder. "Keep it low key. We don't want to spook him. For now just watch anyone he's likely to contact. Maybe we'll get lucky." She hung up.

Based on the reports by the two agents detailing their time of arrival at the house, when Gunderson went missing, the time they spent searching for him, and her best guess at how long it took him to reach the place where the truck picked him up, Marissa estimated he got his ride between 1530 and 1600. She decided to watch that location between those times to see what, if any, trucks might pass. A remote possibility but a possibility she didn't want to miss. Besides, she suspected a West Virginia connection would surface before long and that would help determine her next move.

She slipped into civilian clothes - jeans, sweatshirt and light denim jacket - pulled on her loafers and left the room. Forty-five minutes later she sat in a diner booth across the street from Gunderson's pick-up point, eating a western omelet with onion-laced home fries, washing it down with orange juice and black coffee. The afternoon traffic was pretty light and no trucks appeared in the time window she calculated, even giving herself thirty minutes on either side, so she paid her bill, left a healthy tip and walked out to her van. Marissa sat for a few minutes, reevaluating her approach. She could either return to the area every day for the next week to see if she picked up a trace while she waited for the lab to tell her more about the tire track, or she could head north and start asking questions. She decided that both were studies in futility and that the best use of her time was in poring over his file again.

She found a small clean-looking motel just south of Catawba, chatted with the blue-haired lady behind the desk and got the key to Room 17 at the end of the single row of numbered doors. She showered, slipped into her 'Bama sweatshirt, and spread the thick files out on the king-sized bed.

Marissa leafed quickly through Gunderson's Minnesota childhood but found nothing that would hint at his current destination. As a sophomore at the University of Chicago he developed a system of counting cards while playing Casino that helped him clean out the treasury of four fraternities before word got around. He moved on to small-time cons under six different aliases before graduating to bigger things and hooking up with organized crime in Chicago. What started out as a money laundering operation got out of hand and he skipped town, leaving his bosses to explain themselves. Passing himself off as a math professor, he spent a couple of years in Morgantown. He was apparently quite proficient according to his evaluations. "Looks like he had a future." Marissa smiled and shook her head. She returned the material to the folder and put it away then stretched out on the bed and fell asleep.

The sound of the bedside phone woke her. "Yeah?"

"This is Agent Sharp. The lab says the tire track is probably from a cement truck but it wasn't loaded."

Marissa looked at the clock radio. "It's eight-thirty. Are you working overtime?"

"Ma'am?"

"Shouldn't you be out to dinner?"

"I believe you overslept, Agent Landry. It's eight-thirty AM." Marissa could hear her chuckling.

"I guess I did," she said getting to her feet. "What's happening with Morgantown?"

"We zeroed in on two people, colleagues at the college; older man, retired now and a woman about his age. We have agents keeping track of them round the clock."

"Good. See if you can find that cement truck. I'm going to start easing my way north." She hung up.

Marissa dressed quickly. She never overslept, and she felt like she hadn't slept at all. An image was nagging at her, a shadowy vision of a mountain cabin, and she felt anxious when she tried to bring it into focus. Pushing it away with a firm shake of her head, she hurried to the van and drove to the diner she'd visited yesterday.

Chapter 5

Marissa traced the rim of her coffee cup with a finger. She gazed out the dirt streaked diner window, eyes unfocused, urging her back to her fitful sleep. Despite the anxiety growing inside her, she decided to try and remember more about the dream. Before she could begin to explore it, a loaded cement truck moving south caught her attention with *Catawba Concrete* across the truck's green door in bright yellow gothic font. She signaled for the check and when she paid at the counter, asked the cashier for a local phone book. She found a small display add with a number, an address and a sketchy map to the place. She jotted the info down then spun the open book so it faced the cashier.

"Where are we on this map?" The cashier pointed. Marissa thanked the woman then left.

A few miles north Marissa pulled through the open gates of *Catawba Concrete*. Locating the office, a trailer near the back of the lot, she shut her machine down and stepped out. She climbed the metal steps to the door and raised her arm to knock when the door opened and short chubby man in a checked shirt and jeans almost ran into her.

"Whoa!" he said. "What're you doing here, hon?"

"I'm Special Agent Landry, FBI," she answered, flipping her ID open.

The man stepped back, frowning. "What can I do for you ..." he looked more closely at her ID, "Agent Landry?"

"I believe one of your drivers picked up a hitchhiker day before yesterday around four, a few miles south on 311."

"Drivers ain't allowed to pick up anybody." He stepped around Marissa but she blocked his path.

"This is important, Mr. ..."

"Portella, and my drivers don't pick anyone up."

"How many drivers were on the road at that time?" Portella took a deep breath, frowned and shook his head.

He turned and reached for the door handle. "C'mon inside."

Marissa followed. The office trailer contained a neat row of file cabinets, a copy machine, and a grey metal desk with papers scattered around it. Portella rounded the desk and shuffled through the mess on top. While she waited, Marissa saw a board with nine numbered hooks, six contained sets of keys.

"We had two out that afternoon." He pulled two sheets from the stack. "Al and Marsh. Marsh checked in at ..." he scanned the top sheet. "...at three." He dropped it on the desk and scanned the second. "Al clocked in at four-fifty."

"Where's Al now?"

"He's waiting to load up. He'll tell you the same thing."

"I'm sure, but I'd rather get it first hand." Marissa turned toward the door. "Thanks for your cooperation, Mr. Portella," she said on her way out.

She saw two men standing near a cement truck across the lot and walked toward them. They stopped talking when they noticed her. The shorter one walked away. "Are you Al?" she asked nearing the remaining man.

He nodded. "I'm Marissa Landry, FBI," she said holding out her ID with her left hand and offering her right. Al took it and they shook.

"What can I do for the FBI?"

"I know you're not supposed to pick up hitchhikers and I'm not here to get you in trouble, but we lost a fugitive day before yesterday. It looks like he got a ride around four pm in an unloaded cement truck." Marissa saw his eyes dart in the direction of the office trailer. "Al, just shake your head 'no' while you're telling me where you dropped him. Portella will think you're saying you didn't pick him up."

"What's the fella wanted for?" he asked shaking his head.

"Nothing, but he is a key witness to some bad stuff. Let's not take too much time here." She nodded toward the trailer.

"I dropped him a couple miles north of here, at a strip mall."

"Shake your head harder now and turn away. And thanks." Al followed her direction. Shaking her own head in mock disgust, Marissa turned and hurried to her van, slamming the door when she got in. She started it and kicked up some gravel on the way out.

She drove north, locating the strip mall just over four miles away. She pulled into the lot and parked at the far end under a pin oak. Four stores were occupied; three were vacant. She leaned back in her seat, eyes taking in the names of the functioning businesses, trying to get into Gunderson's head. *Rocky's Pizza, Daniels Optical, Ridge Runner Realtors, and Quick Wash Launderette.* Her brow furrowed. "C'mon Lars, talk to me," she said aloud then it hit her. Marissa hopped out of the van, hurried over to *Ridge Runner Realtors* and walked in.

The lone desk was occupied by a thin middle-aged woman, sharply dressed, with shoulder-length bleached blond hair pulled back from her ears with two silver clips. She looked up when Marissa entered, pasting on a smile when she observed Marissa's faded jeans and worn blazer. "May I help you?"

Marissa extracted her ID. The woman examined it then pasted the smile back on. "How may I help you, Agent Landry?"

Marissa pulled Gunderson's photo from her jacket pocket and handed it to the woman. "Have you seen this man?" The woman glanced at the image then burst out laughing. "Ma'am?"

"Emily," the woman said, shaking her head. "Emily Daniels." Seeing Marissa's confusion she added, "My husband's the optician." She handed the photo back. "I laughed because that guy," she pointed to the photo, "had me baffled. Until now that is."

"How's that, Mrs. Daniels?"

"Emily. Please. He came in a little after four, day before yesterday, looking to buy, he said. Well, he was pretty well dressed, a little disheveled but still … When I asked him where he might want to buy, he ran his finger along the map over there." She pointed to the wall across from her desk where a detailed map depicted the area within a forty-mile radius of the real estate office. The map contained marker pins, some red, most yellow. There were threads attached to the yellow ones, each thread leading to a photo of a house for sale. The northernmost pin was set about thirty miles away near a place called Paint Bank.

"Which home was he interested in?" Marissa asked, knowing the answer.

"The Petri place. That one, way up north."

"Did you take him to look at it?"

"You bet I did. I've been trying to move that one for almost a year."

"What happened?"

"That's the odd part. He looked the place over and seemed genuinely interested, but when I wanted to go back to the office and close the deal, he said he'd want his wife to see it first. I figure, okay because wives buy the houses anyway, hubby just pays the tab."

"Is that it, Emily?"

"Uh uh. We get to the car and he says he wants to be let off at the corner store we passed on the main road. Said he'd have the wife come get him and she could look at the outside. I offered to stick around but he said he was sure he could describe the interior well enough for her to get the idea. Said she loved gardening and the grounds would thrill her. So I left him there." Emily Daniels stood and walked to the map. "I wasted my time, didn't I?"

"I'm afraid so. But you've been really helpful. Thank you." Marissa shook the woman's hand and turned to leave.

"Agent Landry?"

"Yes?"

"Is he even married?"

"Not to my knowledge."

"Damn," Emily Daniels said. Chuckling, she flopped back into her desk chair. Marissa left her there.

Forty minutes later, she parked across 311 from a small corner store. The name on the side street matched the one on the photo of the Petri house. She crossed the road, climbed the two worn wooden steps to a small porch that fronted the place, and went inside. A faded green Formica counter was bracketed by a modern electronic cash register and a refrigerated display case with a sparse assembly of cheeses and lunchmeats. A heavy refrigerator door with a small window in it anchored the back wall. The man behind the counter wore a bloodstained butcher's apron over a white t-shirt and painters pants. What hair he had was cropped close and steel grey. His left arm sported a heart-shaped tattoo pierced by an arrow with a banner inside the heart immortalizing "Rita." A thirty-something couple passed Marissa on their way out, a canvas bag stuffed with their purchases hanging from the man's arm. A teenage boy perused car magazines from a rack on the other side of the store. Marissa waited until the couple left then approached the counter.

"I'd like a turkey and swiss on whole wheat."

"I'm outta wheat. I got seeded rye, white, or pumpernickel."

"Rye." The wall behind the counter contained a few faded photos of the proprietor as a younger man: in a group that looked like family, standing beside a good sized tarpon hung from a crossbar, and with a woman she assumed was "Rita". There were also a couple of photos of a little league team With *Bart's Corner Store* printed in red letters on their yellow shirts. There were various thank you letters from local organizations that *Bart's Corner Store* had supported in some way, a life membership certificate from the NRA, and a series of bills taped on the wall in ascending order from a one to a ten. She noticed two vacant spots that seemed to have once contained bills.

Bart returned with her sandwich and set it on the counter.

"Can I have a ginger-ale?"

"Over there," he nodded toward a cooler near the back of the store. "That'll be four bucks."

Marissa pulled some bills out of her jeans jacket, put four singles on the counter then pointed to the wall. "Looks like there were other bills up there."

He glanced over his shoulder, scowling. "A twenty and fifty. Son-of-a-bitch (pardon my French) stopped in day before yesterday. Ordered a sandwich with pepper-jack cheese. I didn't have any out so I went into the cooler," he nodded toward the heavy door. "When I came out the mo ... SOB was gone along with seventy bucks."

"That's a lot of money to keep on a wall."

"Yeah, I know. I like to tack up the first bill I get in a denomination. Dumb ain't it," he laughed. "You can see I ain't had any hundreds."

Marissa pulled the photo from her pocket. "This the man?"

He nodded. "You his wife or something?"

Marissa smiled. "Agent Landry, FBI." She flashed her ID.

"What'd he do? Besides rob me, I mean."

"He slipped away from two of our agents." She nodded toward the door. "Did you see which way he went?"

"Hell, if I had, I'd have my money back," he shook his head. "Time I saw he wasn't in the store and looked around and seen the money missing, he was long gone. I hightailed it outside but didn't see a trace of him."

"Could he have been picked up?"

Bart pursed his lips. "Don't think so. I'd a heard a car stop." He hesitated then shook his head. "Nope. I don't reckon he was."

"Did he take anything else?"

"He did have a couple of Snicker bars on the counter when he ordered. I guess he took those too." Marissa nodded and turned to leave. "Wait!" he called.

She returned to the counter. "Did you remember something else?"

Bart looked past her. "Hey, Justin! Come over here a minute." The boy put the current *Hot Rod* magazine back on the shelf and shuffled over to the counter, hands stuffed in his pockets, head down. When he reached them, Bart said, "Show him the picture." While Marissa retrieved it from her pocket, he turned toward Justin. "Couple days ago when you come in here and I was hollering about bein' robbed. Remember?" Justin nodded. Marissa put the photo on the counter in front of him. Bart pointed at it. "You see this fella on your way down here?" Justin glanced at the image and shook his head. "You sure?" Justin nodded and Bart slapped the counter hard with both large hands causing Justin and Marissa to flinch.

Marissa picked up the photo. "Justin, did you see anything unusual when you were coming here?" The boy frowned; she watched his eyes. He shook his head. "I'm not sure you're telling me the truth, Justin. I'm an FBI agent ..." Justin glanced at Bart, who nodded, "... and I need to find this man." She showed him Gunderson's picture again. "I believe you can help me."

The boy's eyes widened, his head jerked back and forth as if he were watching a tennis match. He swallowed hard and finally said, "The Duncans."

Marissa looked at Bart. "A couple of bad apples from a farm up the road," he volunteered.

She put a hand on Justin's shoulder. "What about them?"

"I saw a guy get into their truck up the road aways."

"Where was that?"

"Just past Shelter Road." He nodded to the north.

"About a mile up," Bart added.

"Which way were they headed?" He pointed north. "Thank you, Justin. You were a big help."

"He kill somebody?"

"No," Marissa answered, smiling. "I just need to talk to him." The boy nodded. She gestured toward the magazine rack. "Pick one. It's on me." Justin hurried to the rack while Marissa faced Bart. "Where is the Duncan place?"

"About three miles up. Turn right onto Coles Lane. It ends at their farm." He shook his head. "You're gonna want help. Ethan and Artie are a bad pair."

"I'll be careful," she said. Bart, with Justin's help, described the truck while Marissa paid for the latest issue of *Rod and Custom*.

Chapter 6

She didn't see the partially hidden sign heralding *Coles Lane* until she was almost past it. She backed up and eased her van down the rutted one-lane gravel road a little more than a mile, before the leafy canopy opened onto a small clearing with a dirt-streaked mobile home in the center. Marissa pulled off the lane, backing the van around so it faced the road. She thought about retrieving her small snub-nosed thirty-eight from her gun safe, decided against it and opened the door. As she stepped out, the door to the trailer opened a crack, stopped then opened the rest of the way. An overweight, bleach-blond women on the far side of forty appeared, wearing a yellowed T-shirt with no bra underneath, faded baggy jeans, and no shoes. She stood on the top step of the metal staircase and let the door slam. Arms folded across her sagging breasts, she watched Marissa approach. Marissa scanned the clearing, spying a large area completely enclosed in chicken wire that housed several dozen hens, but no sign of other humans.

"Is this the Duncan place?" Marissa asked, stopping several feet away from the steps.

"Who's askin'?"

"Agent Landry, FBI." She produced her ID, holding it open in front of her. "I'm looking for Ethan and Arthur Duncan."

The woman's hands dropped to her sides; she took two steps down and sat hard on the metal stair. "Oh lord! What did they do now?"

"They didn't do anything, ma'am. I just need to talk to them about somebody they may have given a ride to day before yesterday." The woman's face softened.

"Praise Jesus, I thought they'd got themselves into a federal offense." She shook her head. "They're good boys, just a bit wild sometimes. Their daddy died before they was born so I raised them twin boys all alone. Lord knows they needed a daddy, but weren't none." She shook her head again. "Done the best I could."

"I'm sure you did. Are they around?"

"Left this mornin' early in that big old truck of theirs. Ain't been back."

"When do you think they might be back?"

"Couldn't say for sure."

"Mind if I wait?"

The woman frowned. "What was it you wanted to see them about agin?"

"They might have given a ride to a man I'm looking for." The woman nodded.

"Can't see a problem with waitin'." She stood and climbed up the steps. "Like some coffee? It'll grow hair on a turnip, but it's hot."

Marissa nodded.

"C'mon in then." She followed the woman through the door. The odor of fresh-baked bread softened the visual squalor of the interior. The woman shooed a skinny black cat off the cracked vinyl seat of a metal kitchen chair then turned a Dunkin Donuts coffee mug over and filled it from a dented aluminum percolator, returning the pot to the stovetop before passing the cup to Marissa.

Marissa sat in the chair and took a sip. It was every bit as bad as the woman said. She put the cup on the table and waited while the woman shifted some laundry from another chair, merging it with the stack on a third, then sat.

"My name is Alma. I been considerin' goin' back to my maiden name when the boys is out of the house, if they ever leave. It was Monroe, you know like the actress?" She took a long drink of the coffee, shuddered and smiled. "Pretty bad, ain't it?"

"I've had worse," Marissa said. She took another sip. "Did your boys mention anything about giving a ride to someone a couple of days back?"

"Them two never tell me nothin' about what they been up to."

"Maybe you overheard them saying something?" Marissa asked, leaning forward, elbows on the table. "It would be a great help if you could try and remember." Alma nodded. Her eyes narrowed; she sucked in her cheeks until her lips were a tight pucker and stared at a point a foot or so above Marissa's head.

Finally Alma's face brightened. She smiled. "I believe I heard Ethan talking about droppin' a fella." She shook her head. "Didn't say much else, just kept sayin' they dropped the fella and giggling like somebody was twiddlin' his toes."

"He say anything about where?"

"Uh uh." She took another swig of coffee, adding, "Artie started to say something, but Ethan give him a swat back of his head."

Marissa heard the rumble of a barely muffled V-8 in the distance. Alma appeared not to notice it. Taking a last sip of her coffee, she rose. "I'm going to wait outside for the boys, Alma. Thanks for the coffee." She reached the door and turned. "You've been a big help," she said and left Alma sitting at the table.

Outside, she hurried to the van and drove back down the lane hoping to meet the boys at the road. She was about a hundred feet from the end of the lane when the cherry-red GMC pickup turned into it. She eased forward until they were less than ten feet apart then stopped, turned off the engine, applied the parking brake and waited. The twin behind the wheel revved the engine several times then glanced at his brother, said something and shut the engine off. The twins exited the vehicle and stood on either side of the front bumper. They looked to be in their early twenties; both had shaved heads and wore black T-shirts with the sleeves cut off.

Marissa felt the sharp edge of fear poke at her. She could see a scoped rifle and a pump action shotgun resting in a rack across the rear window of the truck. There were no weapons evident on the two young men. She stepped out of the truck, standing with her right hand on the open door within reach of the Glok 40 clamped above the map pocket. "Your mom said you were twins," she said. "I hope she can tell you apart because I bet nobody else can."

The driver crossed in front of the truck and stood next to his brother. Hooking his thumbs in his wide, metal-studded belt, he leaned against the grill, "Who're you, sweet thang?" he asked. His leer made her want a shower.

Marissa produced her ID. "Agent Landry, FBI." She slipped the ID back into her pocket. "Which one of you is Ethan?"

The driver straightened, glanced at his brother, standing with his hands deep in his hip pockets, then said, "Me."

Marissa could smell alcohol. "Ethan, you picked up a hitchhiker day before yesterday, down by Bart's store." She nodded to the south. "I'm interested in knowing where you dropped the person." At the word "dropped" Arthur's eyes flicked toward his brother and a hint of a grin posed on his thin lips before he could stop it.

"We ain't picked up nobody," Ethan said, leaning back against the truck. "What'd this fella do, anyhow?"

"I didn't say it was a man."

Ethan frowned. Arthur pulled his hands from his pockets and sidestepped closer to his brother, arms crossed.

Recovering, Ethan said, "Well, ain't most hitchers men?"

"I really need you to tell me where you dropped the hitcher. I know you picked him up, so cut the BS."

"I don't got to answer no F-B-I questions," he sneered. Arthur nodded his agreement.

"I'm looking for this man and all I want to know is where you left him. If you don't tell me I'll have to arrest you for aiding a fugitive." She could see Ethan weighing his options and hoped the alcohol wasn't going to make him stupid.

"You ain't got no gun," he said, eyes narrowing. He closed the distance between them quickly, fists clenched. Marissa's gut told her Ethan was a bully, mean, but not lethal. She rejected the Glok. Instead she sidestepped his charge and swept his legs out from under him in one smooth motion. On his way down she caught his left hand, pressing her thumb hard against the back of it just above his wrist. She put a foot on his neck and looked up at Arthur, whose eyes were wide. Ethan yelped as she applied pressure with her thumb.

"Now Ethan, where did you leave your hitcher?" Arthur took a step toward her but hesitated when she raised a hand. "If you come at me, I'll have to really hurt your brother in order to stop you. Do you want that?"

121

"Artie," Ethan yelped. "Stay back." Marissa applied more pressure. "OW."

"Yes, Artie. Stay back. Okay Ethan, let's try this again. Where did you drop him?" Applying a bit more pressure to Ethan's hand to punctuate the query, Marissa kept her eyes on Arthur.

Ethan groaned. "About fifteen mile up north there's a dirt road. We left him there."

"Did he say anything while he was with you?" She saw Artie shoot a quick glance at his brother.

"No," Ethan answered. "Now let me the hell up!"

"Artie, is that right?"

He hesitated, eyes dancing. "Uh huh. Feller was quiet as a mouse."

Marissa wondered why they were lying. What benefit would these two get from the lie? One possibility was that Gunderson bought their silence with the money he stole. She rejected that because he needed the money, and he would have known that they couldn't be trusted. The second, far more likely possibility was that they'd mugged him and dumped him.

Marissa pointed to the side of the road with her free hand. "Artie, I want you to walk over there until I tell you to stop." At about fifteen feet, she stopped him. "Okay. Sit down right there, legs out in front and together, hands under your butt." When he hesitated, she twisted Ethan's hand.

"Christ Artie! Do what she says."

When he complied, Marissa looked down at Ethan. "I'm going to take you with me, Ethan." He groaned. "We're going to walk to my van when I let you up. Now, there's about a dozen different ways that I can do real damage to you if you give me any trouble. Do you understand me?" He nodded. "I want you to say it, Ethan."

"I understand."

"Good." Marissa took her foot off his neck, released his arm and stepped away. "Roll onto your back and loosen your belt."

"What the hell?" She stepped toward him. "Okay, okay." He loosened his belt.

"Slide your right arm to your side between your jeans and belt, elbow straight." He complied. "Now pull the belt tight." After helping him to his feet, Marissa walked him toward the van, reaching into her pocket to activate the sliding door as they approached. She checked to make sure Arthur hadn't moved then eased Ethan onto the floor of the van, shackled him to a retaining ring in the floor, his right arm still tethered to his side by the belt.

"Christ! Ya can't haul me around like this."

Marissa closed the door and gave her full attention to the other brother. "I want you to sit there until I'm out of sight then go home."

"Where ya takin' Ethan?" he whined. "Maw,ll wanna know."

"Tell your mom not to worry. She'll get him back in a day or so." She climbed in, started the van and eased it around the red truck. She could see Arthur in the side mirror as she turned onto the paved road. He hadn't moved.

Chapter 7

After a day of questioning back in Richmond, Ethan admitted that he and Artie had been intending to rob Gunderson and dump him. What had happened however, was slightly different from their plan. While they were engaged in cheerful conversation with their quarry Ethan said, "He died." Scared, the two tried to revive Gunderson without success. Finally, they pulled off the road and dumped him. Ethan couldn't remember the exact location. His best recollection put it about twenty miles north of the turnoff to their farm. He said they didn't take anything from the body because they didn't want to be blamed for killing him.

Marissa drove with Ethan in the passenger seat north of the turnoff to the Duncan place for almost thirty miles before he pointed out a ditch where he thought they might have left Gunderson.

"Okay Ethan, out."

"You cain't leave me here!"

"Don't tempt me," she said, pointing to the door. "I want you to show me where you left him, exactly. Now." She watched him slide to the ground and hesitate. "Ethan?" He looked over his shoulder, eyes widening when he recognized a Glok 40 pointed at him. "Please don't try to run." She left her seat and eased across to the passenger side, waving him back with the barrel of the weapon to give her room to exit. "Point to where you put him."

Ethan scanned the area, glancing back several times at the weapon Marissa held at her side. "There," he said, pointing to a hedgerow about thirty feet away. "Right at the end there. Kinda behind it." He turned away from her and took a step toward the spot.

"Stop!" Marissa's sharp order caused him to raise both hands above his head and freeze. She pressed the button that opened the side door. "In," she said. "I worry about you doing something stupid." She cuffed him to the retaining ring, pocketed the Glok then approached the site carefully, looking for sign. The trail was three days cold now; luckily it hadn't rained, but things weren't looking good. She found faint sign that something, animal or human, had lain there. Assuming it was Gunderson, she scouted in ever-widening arcs for any clue as to what happened when or if he woke up from what she assumed based on Ethan's description was another seizure from his shrapnel wound.

Marissa spotted footprints in soft earth more than a hundred feet from the spot. They were from well-worn work shoes, size fourteen at least. Gunderson wore ten. The owner was also much heavier. She squatted on her heels, elbows on her knees and let her eyes drift back and forth among the half-dozen prints. She breathed rhythmically, freeing her mind. Several minutes later, she noticed that a couple of the prints were deeper than the rest, not much, but definitely deeper.

Standing, Marissa looked toward the hedgerow. It was possible to see a body from where she stood. It would be more visible from the road, just a few feet away. The shoulder was paved so she didn't bother to examine it, instead she returned to the van and Ethan.

"It's about damn time. These things hurt." Marissa smiled and closed the side door, muffling his litany of complaints. She circled the machine and climbed behind the wheel. "Hey! Wait! You cain't leave me here!"

"Watch me." She slipped the Glok from her waistband, clipping it into the door holster before starting the van.

Sure that she wasn't going to get any more information from Ethan, she drove him back to Coles Lane, hearing his complaints the entire thirty miles. She left him at the turn, letting him walk the mile to the farm.

On her way back to the motel, she wondered if any unidentified corpses had turned up at local hospitals or mortuaries. If Gunderson was dead, her work was done. In her gut, she didn't think he was. When Marissa entered her room, the message light on the phone was flashing. The card attached to the under side of the phone instructed her to call the front desk. She dialed '0' and let it ring five times before hanging up and walking across the courtyard to the door marked *Office*. The room was empty, but she could hear a TV behind the closed door on the other side of the reception desk. A sign on the counter read *Ring for service* with an arrow pointing to a button embedded in the counter top. Marissa pressed the button and heard a loud buzzer from the closed room. The TV went silent. Soon the door opened and a tall man in his sixties emerged, rubbing his eyes.

"Sorry, I musta dozed watching the tube." He placed both hands flat on the countertop. "What can I help you with?"

"There was a message for me. Room seventeen?"

The clerk turned to a box on the wall, retrieved a pink sheet of paper and handed it to her. She thanked him and left. On the way across the courtyard she read. "Call home." Marissa veered away from the room and out to the street, crossing to the diner. She ordered coffee at the counter then headed for the wall phone in the restroom alcove. She punched in her access code then Harvey's number.

"Delancey."

"Hi Harvey. You called?"

"How's everything going in the mountains?"

126

"Okay." Marissa waited for him to get to the reason for his message.

"Drop it for now. I need you back at the shop."

"What's up?"

"Kidnapping. Domestic."

"Why me?"

"Guy's a survivalist. Took his ex into the Smokey's. Left her vehicle by the roadside. Dogs lost his trail."

Marissa sighed. "How long ago?"

"Yesterday. His file will be waiting for you."

"Okay. Oh and find out if any unidentified bodies showed up at morgues around Paint Bank, Virginia, last few days." She hung up, paid for the coffee and left. In number seventeen, she packed up Gunderson's file and her clothes. Tossing everything in the van, she crossed to the office to settle her bill.

Chapter 8

After an hour of heated discussion, Delancey agreed to hold off assigning backup until she located the kidnapper. Marissa promised to call for the backup before making contact.

She tracked the pair across twenty miles of impossible terrain, losing the trail for hours at a time. Often, a tiny piece of fabric, or a drop of blood, was the only sign of their passing. By the time she located them in a remote cabin high over Cherokee, North Carolina, Marissa felt angry and afraid – afraid for the woman, but more than that. She felt tightness in her gut, a feeling of near panic she hadn't experienced since waking up in the hospital more than a decade ago. Her fingers found the long scar on her neck. She wanted very badly to take this beast down hard, but at the same time knew she couldn't do it alone without getting the woman killed. She hurried into town and called Delancey.

"I located them." Ignoring his congratulations, she continued. "I need a sniper, ASAP." Having met a few FBI snipers, she added, "And I don't want any gung-ho trigger-happy kid."

"Got it, Missy Mae. Where are you?" She gave him the location of the cabin, hung up the pay phone and headed back into the hills to watch and wait.

Four hours later, she reacted to a slight rustle of brush on her left, spinning to face the sound, Glok ready. She saw nothing.

"Don't shoot, Agent Landry." The voice, a whisper, came from behind her. She turned to see a tall man in camouflage leaning against an oak sapling, a fifty-caliber rifle slung over his shoulder, muzzle down. A shock of wavy grey hair spilled from under his cap and his pleasant smile accentuated the lines on his weathered face.

128

"JT Marshall," he whispered, extending his hand. "Call me JT."

She shook it. "Marissa." She motioned to the cabin set in the middle of a clearing a hundred-fifty-yards away. "They haven't been out of the place since I came back up."

"You sure they're still in there?"

She nodded. "I saw movement a while back."

"Him or her?"

"Him, I think. I couldn't get close enough to be sure."

JT unslung his weapon, opened and locked the bipod, assumed a prone position and pointed the rifle at the cabin. He flipped the caps open on the scope and looked through it, adjusting the focus. "I see her. She's sitting on a cot. Can't see him."

"Is she restrained?"

"Can't tell."

"How does she look?"

"Tired. Split lip. Breathing is regular. She's looking to her left, toward the door." JT rested the rifle butt on the ground and rose, squatting on his heels. "How do you want to handle this?"

Marissa squatted beside him. "Personally, I'd like you to blow his head off. I saw photos of her taken at the hospital when she finally left the bastard. I guess he wasn't done with her yet." She shook her head. "Domestics are impossible to predict. We ought to try doing this without getting anyone killed, but my primary concern is for the woman. If we can't do it any other way, he's yours."

JT nodded. "When?"

"Let's see if he comes out, so we can separate them." Marissa pointed to a spot to the right of the cabin. "I can get closer there than anywhere else. No window on that side." She swept the ground in front of her free of debris. "The place has three windows, one in back, one on the south side, and the one you see." She sketched the floor plan of the cabin while she spoke. "The windows are pretty small, somebody might squeeze through but it would take time, so logically the door is his only egress." She sat back on her heels.

"Tunnel a possibility?"

Marissa shook her head. "From the northwest corner - the ground slopes there - I had room to slide under a bit. The floor's solid. " She continued, "I can get right up against the north wall. He'll have to leave at some point, maybe we'll get lucky and he'll use the facilities." She drew a box in the dirt to locate the small outhouse in her sketch. "When he does, I'll go in."

"You won't be able to see him from the north side."

"No, but you will." Reaching into her pack, she retrieved two small radios complete with ear buds, tossing one to JT. She slipped into the brush without a sound.

Marissa made a wide circle around the ridge and arrived at the north wall thirty minutes after leaving JT. Up at the spot where they'd parted, she saw only the forest. Frowning, she realized she'd made a rookie mistake, heading out before they checked the radios. She looked up the hill and tapped the earphone.

"I got you, Marissa. No worries." She flashed a thumbs-up.

An hour and a half later JT said, "Door's opening." Marissa drew her sidearm. "Just him. Heading for the firewood." She nodded, picturing the woodpile in her mind, about fifty feet from the door. She waited.

"Got him an armload and coming back."

Marissa stepped out, assumed a firing position. "Freeze, FBI!"

The man stopped. "You it?"

"No asshole," Marissa answered, "I just tagged you. You're it. Put the wood down. Now!" He let the load roll off his arms. "Hands behind your head!" He obeyed, smiling.

"Want me on my knees, missy? That's the drill, ain't it?"

Marissa fought a twinge of fear. She held her weapon steady. "Do it!" The man knelt.

He raised his head staring at her with cold green eyes. "What's next, little missy?"

Before she could answer, she heard "Knife!" in her ear and the man's head exploded. As the body fell, she saw that its right hand gripped a half-sheathed hunting knife.

Her hand shook as she holstered her weapon and turned toward the cabin.

JT was at her side before she reached the open door. His rifle was slung over his left shoulder; his right hand, hanging relaxed at his side, held a 9mm automatic. He took a position to the left of the door.

Marissa drew her weapon. Stepping to the right side of the door, she called "FBI, ma'am. You're safe now." She waited a tic then added, "You can come out now."

The woman appeared in the light of the doorway, saw the body that once was her captor, and collapsed.

Chapter 9

Two months later, Marissa walked into Harvey Delancey's office and sat in the chair next to his desk. "How you feeling, Missy Mae?"

"You saw the report; shrink says I'm fine."

"I know what the report says. I'm asking you."

"I'm good, Harv." She leaned forward in her chair. "I still don't see why you thought I needed all that time off."

"I know, hon."

"Tell me. Why?"

Delancey sighed. "JT saw things out there that troubled him, and I trust his judgment." He looked at her for a long couple of seconds then added, "Want the details?" She shook her head.

Marissa frowned. "You didn't call me in to ask about my mental health," she said, leaning forward. "Why am I here?"

"Got some news for you, Missy Mae."

"Shoot."

"Gunderson."

Marissa straightened. "I'm listening."

Delancey pushed a file toward her. "Seems he now has a bank account."

She scanned the single sheet then closed the folder. "Only deposits?" Delancey nodded. "The bank's quite a way from where the Duncan boys left him," she added. He nodded again. "How'd he get there, I wonder?"

"That's what I pay you the big bucks for," he said, handing her the folder. "Go get him."

Milo's Gift

Marissa rose, scooted around the corner of the desk, planted a quick kiss on top of his bald head, and left. On her way down to the parking garage she tried to figure out why Gunderson opened a bank account under his own name. It didn't make any sense. He was too careful, too smart. She sat in her van for over an hour trying to get her head around it. Finally, she left the garage and drove west on US 60, toward the Blue Ridge Mountains. With no particular urgency to pick up the months-old trail, she preferred the meandering route to the more direct interstate. That evening, Marissa treated herself to a room at the Hampton Inn in Lexington, delighting in the feel of the old hotel, so different from the new buildings bearing that corporate name.

Chapter 10

The following morning after her normal yoga routine, Marissa abandoned her usual jeans and T-shirt, opting for a lime-green lightweight turtleneck, grey slacks and jacket with black loafers. She tied her long honey-blond hair into a ponytail with a silk scarf that matched her shirt. After assessing the result in the mirror, she drove north to Luray - a sleepy little town whose claim to fame is a huge hole in the ground that bears its name. She arrived at *Luray Savings and Loan* around eleven.

There were two teller windows, one open, but no customers. The only other person in the bank sat behind a huge desk in the windowed southeast corner of the room. It took a minute before she realized that the ornate carving on the modesty panel of the desk announced *President – Luray Savings and Loan*. Wearing her most pleasant smile, she approached the desk and the small, thirtyish balding man behind it. He rose as she neared, returning her smile while his eyes engaged in a quick head-to-toe scan. He stepped around the desk, extending his right hand and indicating the chair next to the desk with his left. She shook his hand and sat, crossing her legs, left over right.

"My name is Roy Butler, miss … ?"

"Landry," she answered, leaning forward.

"How may I help you Miss Landry?"

"Mr. Butler, I'm looking for a fugitive …" When he looked puzzled, she gave him a self-deprecating grin. "Oh, I'm sorry Mr. Butler." She produced her badge. "I'm an FBI agent. I sometimes forget that people don't automatically know that. Silly of me." She shrugged.

He seemed unsure whether to smile again or become soberly businesslike, finally settling on a quizzical smirk. "Perfectly alright," he said. "Is this someone you're looking for a customer of our bank?"

134

"Yes, he has a savings account here." She produced Gunderson's photo.

Butler didn't take his eyes off Marissa. "I'm not the one you should show this to. I rarely have personal contact with depositors. I'm sure one of our tellers would be able to help you," he said loud enough to carry to their cages.

"Thank you, Mr. Butler." Marissa rose. Butler stood, once again offering his hand, which she shook, holding it a second longer than necessary. She approached the first brass-barred window and showed the grey-haired woman behind it Gunderson's photo. Giving the teller his name and account number, she explained that he was a fugitive she was looking for.

The woman typed the number on her keyboard then shook her head. "Lord, no. The gentleman who set the account up is much older than that, and not nearly so clean-shaven, or clean in general for that matter." The woman leaned close to the bars. "He smelt a bit like a barn, dontcha know."

A little confused, Marissa asked, "Do you have a photo of the man on your screen?"

"No."

"How is it you know what …?"

"Oh, I associate faces with deposits. It's my way of remembering my customers."

Marissa nodded. "How often does this man come in?"

"Well, it's not like clockwork, but he does show up within a few days of the first of the month." She thought a minute then added, "Never more than a week off, he is."

"Does he show up at any particular time of day?"

"Mid-afternoon, generally. Around two, two-thirty. About then."

"Never earlier?"

"Not since I've worked here, and that's going on forty-five years."

"He's been coming here that long?"

"Why, no." The teller chuckled. "It's been maybe thirteen, fourteen years."

"Is there ever anyone else with him?" The woman shook her head. "When was the last time he showed up?"

The woman tapped a few keys then answered, "June 5th. It being the end of June now, I'd expect him within the next six or seven days. Of course we'll be closing on the fourth, but we'll be opening back up, day after."

"Thank you very much for your time," Marissa said, turning to leave. She stopped after a few steps and faced the teller. "Does he bring the money in cash or checks?"

"Oh, no. He transfers it from another account."

Marissa returned to the teller's window. "So you have his name?"

"Why I'm sure it's in our files, but the account isn't in his name." She tapped a few more keys. "It belongs to a Jennifer Benedict." She nodded in the direction of the president. "I believe Mr. Butler would have more information about how all that is set up." She unlatched the window. Swinging it aside and leaning through, she yelled "Hey Roy! Can you help Miss ..." she squinted at Marissa.

"Landry."

"… Miss Landry?" She smiled at Marissa and retreated into her booth. "That's my son, Roy. Doesn't he look distinguished?"

Marissa thanked the teller again then made her way back to the president's desk. He stood, motioning to the chair.

"Sorry to bother you again, Mr. Butler," she said, sitting in the worn leather chair. "But it seems I need to find out some details about Ms. Jennifer Benedict."

Rising, he buttoned his suit jacket and turned to face the quintet of four-drawer file cabinets behind his desk. He opened the second drawer from the top on the left-most cabinet and flipped through the index tabs on the hanging folders, mumbling names as he did. Retrieving one, he returned to the desk, unbuttoned his jacket, sat on the edge of his large chair, and opened the folder. "Ah, yes. Miss Jennifer Benedict. What do you need to know?"

"Who is the man managing her account?"

He leafed through a few pages. "Hmm … yes, here it is." Butler lifted a single sheet, perusing it at length before handing it to Marissa. It was a power of attorney authorizing Mr. J. Pardon Soames to act on behalf of Miss Jennifer Benedict in all financial matters. The document was drawn up and notarized in a Roanoke law office of *Parson and Page* ten years ago.

"Did Miss Benedict open the account in person?"

He leafed through a few more sheets. "Yes she did."

"So you've met her then?"

"Oh no. The account was opened twelve years ago, when my father was in this chair."

"So your father is retired?"

"He passed six years back."

"I'm sorry."

Roy Butler nodded. Gripping the padded arms of the high-backed chair, he slid fully into it, almost disappearing in the process. Marissa couldn't help wondering if his feet were actually touching the floor. "He left the bank and the house to Mama." He glanced in the direction of the teller's cage, flashing a brief smile. Marissa resisted the impulse to turn, sure she'd see the woman leaning over the counter. "Mama likes chatting with everyone who comes in so she made me president and stayed on in her window."

"She would have met Miss Benedict then, I imagine."

"I doubt it. Daddy would have handled the initial deposit from here."

Marissa leaned forward, lowering her voice to just above a whisper. "Mr. Butler, I know this is a little irregular, but ..." she hesitated long enough for him to slide forward and lean his arms on the desk, covering the folder. "May I ask the amount of the initial deposit?" She touched his hand as she spoke.

Coloring, Butler picked up another sheet. "Twenty-one thousand three hundred and eighty-four dollars and thirty-eight cents." He passed the sheet across the desk.

Marissa stared at the Xerox copy of a U.S. Treasury check. "May I have a copy of this file?" she asked, handing it back.

"Of course." He collected the papers, rose and disappeared behind the teller station, returning a few minutes later with the copies. He opened a bottom drawer in his desk, produced a manila folder and slipped the copies inside. Marissa thanked him and rose to leave.

"Glad we could help our federal law enforcement agency," he said. He stepped around the desk, extending his hand. Marissa took it, noticing that he glanced past her frowning. The frown quickly morphed into a pleasant smile. "Miss Landry, or should I call you Agent Landry?"

"Either one is fine." She released his hand.

"Mama and I would be pleased if you'd join us for dinner this evening."

Marissa grinned. "I'm sorry Mr. Butler. I have to leave right away, but thank you, and your mother, for the kind offer." She turned, nodding to the teller/owner and left the building. She identified herself at the *Page County Sheriff's Office* on Court Street, faxed the file to Harvey then got back on the road, heading south to Roanoke.

Chapter 11

The offices of *Parson and Page* occupied a storefront in the middle of a seedy side street between Centre and Shenandoah, close enough to the rail yard to hear the clank and clatter of freight cars rolling by. A heavy woman with short, curly hair, dyed strawberry blonde, sat behind a gunmetal grey desk just inside the door, her fingers poised above the keys of an IBM Selectric typewriter.

"May I help you?" she asked.

Marissa produced her ID. "I'd like to see one of the partners."

The woman punched a button on her phone and picked it up. "Mr. Page, there's an FBI agent here to see you." She hung up the phone. "He'll be right out. Have a seat." She indicated a row of four vinyl and steel chairs, divided by an artificial Ficus tree. Marissa sat in the chair nearest the closed office door. A moment later it opened and a tall man in a well-worn blue pinstriped suit stepped through. Marissa pegged him to be in his late fifties. His steel grey eyes, shock of white hair and pleasant smile invited one to trust him. Reminding herself he was a lawyer, she subdued the feeling. She stood.

"Mr. Page, I'm Agent Marissa Landry, FBI." She shook his hand.

He stepped away from the door motioning her in. "What can I do for you, Agent Landry?" he said, closing the door behind them.

Marissa fished the power-of-attorney from the folder. "I'd like some help with this," she said, handing it to him.

"May I see your identification?" She produced her badge and ID. Page ignored the badge, examining the ID instead. Satisfied, he perused the paper she'd handed him. "My office did this. Is there a problem?" He handed it back.

"No, but I'm investigating another matter and Ms. Benedict is an integral part of it. I was wondering if you could help me locate her."

"I'm afraid not. Attorney-client privilege."

"If she was who I was investigating, I'd absolutely agree with you Mr. Page, but she's not. I have no interest in her in that way."

Page smiled and shook his head. "That won't wash, Agent Landry. Sorry." He glanced at his watch. "I have a client coming in a few minutes and I have a bit more preparation to attend to." He walked to the door, opened it and stepped aside. "Please excuse me, Agent Landry. Sorry I couldn't be more help."

I'm sure you are, Marissa thought returning his smile. She said, "Until we meet again," on her way out the door.

Chapter 12

"Tilting at windmills, are we Missy Mae?" Harvey said with a chuckle Marissa could hear clearly through the phone. "You didn't seriously think you'd get any information from a lawyer did you?"

"Thought I'd give it a shot. I'm going to move my base up to Luray and wait for Mr. Soames to show. I'll have the bank call me when he comes in."

"Can you make that happen without alerting him?"

Marissa sighed. "It may cost me an incredibly uncomfortable evening meal, but I'm pretty sure I can." She hung up.

The next morning she checked in to a Best Western at the edge of Luray. After notifying Harvey and changing clothes, she drove into town and parked down the block from the bank. A brief conversation with President Butler and his mother, and an agreement to have dinner with them the following evening, yielded a plan to have Roy Butler signal Soames' arrival by simply walking out of the bank and down to the coffee shop on the corner. The plan was complicated by the fact that he didn't know what the man looked like, so his mother said she would indicate the man's presence by coughing three times as soon as he walked through the door.

"What if you have to cough when someone else walks in?" Marissa had asked.

"Oh, Mama never coughs," Roy offered. "She does have this funny little way of sneezing however." He turned toward his mother then and, despite Marissa's assurance that she was satisfied, Mama emitted three cat-like sneezes.

Outside, Marissa hurried to her van. She drove to her motel where she changed into her work clothes, jeans and T-shirt. After a quick lunch at a small café across the street from her lodgings, she drove back to the bank, parking her van in the shade of a building a block away but within sight of the front door. She left after the Butlers locked up for the day.

The following afternoon she stationed her van in the same place at twelve-thirty and settled back in her seat to wait. While she waited, Marissa tried to assess the meaning of the troubling dreams that she'd been having for the past few days. The spotty details she could recall, a cabin, a smokehouse, a pit filled with ashes and shards of bone. They troubled her, less because of the bizarre elements of the dreams than because, somewhere in her mind she sensed they were a memory rather than a symbolic fabrication.

While she was trying to allow her mind to go to that place, an ancient International Scout parked across the street from the bank, and a massive old man climbed out. The side buttons on his faded bib overalls were undone and his stained red T-shirt had the arms cut out, freeing his powerful shoulders. He wore scuffed work boots laced all the way up, the drooping loops of the bows and the ends of the laces, peaking out from the legs of the overalls. He had the long stride of one who walked more than rode. Seconds after he entered the bank, Roy Butler strode through the door, hurrying across the street with a contrived casualness that made Marissa smile. Fifteen minutes later, J. Pardon Soames left the bank and drove off with Marissa following at a discreet distance. Roy Butler had not come out of the coffee shop by the time she left.

The thing Marissa first noted about Soames' vehicle after its age was the license plate. It was muddy enough that she couldn't get a number, but the state was West Virginia. She kept him in sight, sometimes as much as half a mile away, other times much closer as they passed through tiny towns, when possible with at least one other vehicle between them. Three-and-a-half hours after they left Luray, Soames turned into a road that was nothing more than a pair of ruts left by years of tractors. Marissa drove past it without slowing because she knew that there was no way to continue the tail undetected, but also because she felt tense and anxious, and afraid. She made a U-turn a bit farther on and drove back to Luray to steel herself for dinner with the Butlers.

Chapter 13

The next morning, Marissa rose before dawn to prepare for the trip into the backcountry of West Virginia. As she drove, she pushed her rising anxiety away, labeling it a product of her dreams. Instead, she reviewed the previous night's dinner, admitting first that the widow Butler was an excellent cook, second that Roy Butler would be forever tied to his mother's apron, and third that she actually enjoyed herself.

Marissa turned the van onto an old logging road a few hundred yards beyond Soames' turnoff. A quarter mile up the rutted road, she pulled off behind a stand of young white pine and shut it down. She packed enough provisions into the pockets of her cargo pants and small backpack to be out for several days. Adding a sheathed K-bar knife to her belt, she locked the machine and bushwhacked her way through the woods to the tractor path. Soames' place would be somewhere ahead.

Twenty minutes later, Marissa spotted a game trail on the left and froze. She stared at the barely visible break in the underbrush, anxiety building, threatening to take hold of her. She fought for control with every meditative trick she'd learned, until finally her breathing and heartbeat had slowed to acceptable levels. When she allowed herself back into the present, she was startled to feel her hand caressing the long scar on her throat. She took one more long, cleansing breath then stepped off the tractor path and onto the trail and made her way down a steep narrow track into a ravine. The tiny stream at the bottom of the ravine flowed west-southwest. Marissa crossed to the other side and picked her way up and along the rim for a little over a mile before it made a sharp turn, landing her at a narrow dirt road. It meandered through old growth forest climbing steadily for another two miles. When Marissa caught the faint odor of gasoline, she left the road for the cover of the heavy undergrowth. She spotted an

145

unpainted shed, its double doors hanging wide open on bent, rusted hinges. She heard a woman's voice coming from the interior and closed to a point that allowed her a good view while remaining hidden. An old Jeep, partially hidden in the shadow of the building overhang, rested on heavy wooden blocks, its tires a few inches off the ground. Edging closer to the open door she listened.

"The Buick's mine. After Carl brought me here and locked me up, he went through my purse and got the keys." Marissa's heart lept. Calming herself she continued to listen. "… got the car and brought it here. I'm guessing with Jethro." Marissa felt the new name push at her consciousness. "… brought me here to show me. He said, 'Won't nobody be lookin' for you bitch.' I had actually thought someone would notice the car abandoned and start a search, or something. 'Won't nobody be lookin' for you bitch,' he said. Then good old Carl the bastard Larson bent me over the hood of my own car and sodomized me." Marissa stifled a gasp. Backing away, she slipped quickly and silently deep into the woods and threw up until there was nothing left.

Marissa lay on her side, knees tight to her chest and bit her lip until it bled, hoping the pain would keep her from screaming. She clutched her neck with both hands over her scar.

Chapter 14

Marissa's eyes snapped open. The hand reaching for her hesitated, giving her an advantage, and she took it. Grabbing the hand, her fingers around the meaty part of the thumb, finger tips in its palm, she pressed her own thumb on the back of the hand and twisted.

"Ow!" howled the hand's owner as she rolled him across her body and straddled him. The young boy, eyes wide, struggled to free himself.

Marissa put more pressure on his hand, hissing, "Stop squirming and I'll let you up." She eased the hold a little when the boy's struggles subsided. "I'm going to let you up as soon as you relax, and I want to talk with you when I do." She eased her grip a little more. "Understand?" The boy nodded then became still. Marissa held on a moment longer then rose and released his hand.

As soon as she stepped back, he sprang to his feet facing her, reached behind his back and drew a knife. Marissa watched his eyes. When he lunged, knife hand forward, she sidestepped like a matador and disarmed him with a blow to his wrist, twisted his arm behind him and pressed him against a large oak tree. "Dammit boy! I don't want to hurt you but you've got to take it easy. You hear me?"

"Uh huh," he answered. Marissa released him and stepped back, ready. The boy faced her and leaned against the tree, rubbing his wrist, his eyes darting side to side.

"Don't even think about it," she warned.

He stared at her then, cocking his head, he scanned her from head to toe. "Y'all ain't from around here."

Marissa had to smile. "No, I'm not. My name's Marissa. What's yours?"

The boy frowned. His eyes told her he was trying to remember something. Finally, he refocused on her face; still frowning, he straightened. "Milo Larson." Marissa paled but held herself in check. "You okay, ma'am?" She nodded, took a long breath and another step backward. She could see the resemblance, a little. The high cheekbones and jutting jaw, finer features than his father ... she forced herself to remain calm. "Yer lookin' at me funny," he said, fidgeting.

"Sorry ... sorry, Milo." She forced a smile. She needed to know about ... "You live near here?" she asked.

"Less'n a mile yonder." He pointed in the direction of the garage she'd left.

Marissa nodded, continuing to smile. "With your folks?"

"Maw 'n Robert," he offered. "Paw's gone."

She felt a chill but steadied herself. "Where did he go?" Milo looked away then back at her. "Milo?"

"Don't rightly know, ma'am. He wus there then he wadn't."

She let his answer settle for a few seconds then asked, "How long ago was that?"

"Mebbe, ten – 'lebben year. A long while."

"And he hasn't ever been back?" Milo shook his head. Marissa found her breath coming more easily. She relaxed enough to notice that the sun was low on the horizon. "Milo, it's getting late. You probably want to get home. I have a favor to ..."

"Ain't goin' home."

"Why?"

"'Cus Maw wants us t' leave with Mr. Robert." He shook his head violently. "I ain't goin', nohow."

Marissa let that sink in before asking, "But where else will you go?" Milo swept the air with both hands. "You mean live in the woods?" He nodded. "But you need to have shelter." Milo motioned for her to follow then slipped silently into the forest.

She grabbed his knife from the ground, slipped it into her utility belt and hurried after him onto a narrow game trail that wound higher up the mountain. Twenty minutes of steady climbing led them to a cave opening under a rock ledge, invisible until they were within a few feet of the mouth. She followed Milo inside. She assessed the interior while he assembled a small fire on the north edge of the entrance. The area was about ten feet deep by eight high and wide, narrower at the mouth, maybe five feet.

Milo struck two stones together a few times then blew on the tinder to encourage the small flame. Marissa watched his sure hands arranging the dry hardwood over the kindling. When he'd finished, the fire was small, smokeless and adding warmth to the cave. He sat back, leaning against the wall, a proud smile on his face. Marissa nodded her approval, grinning. They watched the growing shadows fade into darkness as the sun dropped behind the mountain.

Milo rose and started for the entrance. Marissa put out an arm to stop him. "Need wood," he said. "Rain tomorrow." He pointed toward the sliver of sky visible in the entrance.

She nodded. "Okay. Let's go." They retraced their steps a short way down the path then Milo veered right and disappeared into the brush. Marissa hurried to catch up, saw him a short distance away and slowed her step to just keep him in sight. He stopped a minute or so later, waiting until she reached him. They were in a small clearing bracketed by two dead maples. Milo snapped several limbs off, breaking them into smaller pieces with his bare foot. When he was satisfied, he gathered the pieces in his arm. Marissa held hers out so he dumped his load in her arms and restocked his own. She followed him back to the game trail and up to the cave. Inside, they dumped the wood in a pile against the back wall. Milo reached into a crevice near the woodpile and withdrew an army-green ammo box. He opened it and extracted two biscuits and several strips of jerky. He handed one biscuit and a piece of the jerky to Marissa. She took a bite of the meat.

The taste of the dried venison snapped her back to the smokehouse. She could feel leather biting into her wrists, feel her arms stretching under her weight, feel the sting of the willow switch on her back and buttocks.

"You okay, ma'am?" Milo was kneeling above her. "Wus the meat bad?"

She smelled her own fear. She tried to control her breathing, inhaling in great, gasping gulps until she thought she could speak. Milo looked near panic. "I ... I'm okay, Milo. This happens sometimes." She smiled and touched his face with her trembling fingers. "I'll be fine. I just need to catch my breath."

"Y'all cold? I c'n build up the fire."

She shook her head and put a hand on his shoulder to steady herself. "May I have another piece of that jerky?" Looking relieved, Milo hurried back to his stash in the crevice. Returning with two pieces, he held them out. Marissa took one, hesitated a second then bit into it. When she finished that piece she searched around for the biscuit, finding it near the cave entrance. She snapped the rock-hard cake in two and took a bite. Stale as it was, she ate it all then took the other strip of jerky from Milo and ate that.

When they'd eaten their fill, Milo closed and sealed the box, sliding it back into its crevice. He pulled on a bundle in the shadows, emerging with what looked like a small bear but revealed itself to be a series of animal skins well tanned and sewn together. When he noticed Marissa watching, Milo grinned. "They's all critters I snared. Done tanned the hides and put'em t'gether my own self."

"Excellent work, Milo."

"Maw, taught me the sewin', 'n Paw the snarin'." Marissa worked hard to keep from shaking.

She pushed a smile forward. "I bet they're proud of you."

"Maw, fer shore. Don't know 'bout Paw. It's like I said …"

"Yes, I remember," she interrupted. "It's getting late and I have a long day ahead." She hesitated before asking, "May I bunk here?" Milo smiled and nodded.

"Y'all kin use this," he said, offering the skins. "Gits right chilly up here."

"I'm fine, Milo." She pulled a thin foil blanket from a pocket and a wallet-sized item with a knob on one corner. She opened the valve and it slowly unfolded, filling with air until it lay flat on the floor about a yard long and half a yard wide. She closed the valve. When she looked at Milo, his eyes were saucers.

"It just fills up with air, Milo. Nothing fancy."

"But y'all didn't blow in it. It just done it."

"It's hard to explain, Milo." She smiled. "Good night."

Milo's Gift

Milo wrapped himself in the hides. "G'night, ma'am."

She could now smell the coming rain in the night air.

Chapter 15

Marissa woke tired from a night filled with fitful dreams. When she opened her eyes, Milo was gone. "Damn!" She bolted upright, scrambling to the cave entrance. The shadows told her it was nearly 0800. She beat her fists on the walls, punishing herself for her inattention. "Where the hell did he go?" she growled. She pressed the air out of her mattress and slipped it in her pocket along with the blanket then left the cave. Rounding the first turn on her way down, she saw Milo. He was loping up the trail with a dead rabbit, gutted and bleeding, hanging from his right hand. Her hand went to her utility belt. The knife was missing.

Milo saw her and held out the rabbit as he approached. "Breakfast," he said. Noticing her hand on her belt, he added, "Sorry, ma'am. Ah needed m' knife."

Marissa nodded. "I'll make a fire while you skin it." They returned to the cave together.

She built a small, hot fire using her lighter and a cotton ball saturated with petroleum jelly, getting another wide-eyed stare out of Milo. He skinned the rabbit and impaled it on a sturdy stick then sat cross-legged in front of the fire, his full attention on the meat while Marissa sat in the shadows in full lotus, eyes closed.

After breakfast, they sat leaning against opposite walls, eyeing each other.

"Milo, I need to ask a favor."

He frowned. "Whut?"

"I need to make sure nobody knows I'm here."

"You runnin' from the law?"

Marissa saw the excitement in his face. "Sort of," she lied. "So you can't tell anybody I'm hiding here."

"I bet Jethro'd hep. He don't truck with the law a'tall." Milo nodded, smiling. "Told me so hisself."

"No Milo," she said. "Don't let anybody know. It has to be our secret. Understand?"

Disappointment showed on his face. "Nobody?"

"Nobody." She stood and walked over to him then knelt, putting her hands on his shoulders. "Promise me, Milo." She watched his face change while he evaluated his alternatives. Finally he nodded. "Promise." She could see he meant it.

Letting go of his shoulders she moved beside him, resting her back against the stone. "Milo, when did Robert arrive at your farm?"

"He dint perzakly arrive. I done found'm in Skunk Holler, daid. Well, not really daid, but he shore looked it. Maw knew he wadn't though and we hauled him up, least ways Rosie hauled him up, then we put'm on the stone-boat 'n Rosie hauled that t' the farm. Maw took all his clothes, 'ceptin' his drawers. She looked Mr. Robert over real good, she did, she bein' one time a nurse. Couldn't see nothin' 'cept some mark on his neck - back here." Milo indicated a point near the base of his skull.

"Milo," Marissa said, touching his forearm. "What I really wanted to know is, when did all that happen?"

"Oh." He nodded then closed his eyes, nodding his head as if marking a count of some kind. "'Twas late spring, about two - three month back. Yep, that's it."

They sat side-by-side listening to the rain. Marissa reassessed Milo's shelter. Many of the larger crevices in the rugged walls housed metal containers like the one holding the food stores while others held fabric and burlap bundles tied with rawhide. The overhanging ledge at the mouth of the cave kept rainwater out while clear cold water dribbled from a crack in the back wall, losing itself in a small, sandy pool. *A perfect little home*, she though and wondered whether he'd found it on his own or had his daddy introduced him to it. She found herself able to bring up Carl's image without panicking. Outside the rain had stopped.

Pulling her knees up to her chin, Marissa planted her feet flat on the floor and stood. "Milo, will you show me where Jethro lives?" she said, turning to face the boy. He nodded and rose, hurrying toward the cave mouth. She put a hand on his arm. "Easy. I want to do it without him knowing we're there." Milo nodded again. The conspiratorial grin that crossed his face, made Marissa smile. He led the way down the mountain.

About halfway down the game trail leading back to his own home, Milo stopped. Marissa put a hand on his shoulder, turning him. Her eyes asked the question. He opened his mouth but she put a finger to her lips, shaking her head. Milo nodded. He pointed to his ear and then to a point about ten-o'clock. Marissa caught the sound then, listened for a few seconds then smiled. "Bear, foraging for acorns," she whispered. Seeing his frown she added, "Sniff the air." Watching him pick up the faint scent, she grinned. "Sounds like there are two of them, cubs I'd guess. They don't stink like momma." Milo listened some more then nodded and walked on. A short distance past the point where they'd had their first meeting, Milo pointed right and turned that way. They skirted a clearing that was now familiar to Marissa as her memories kept lining up, triggered by the sights, sounds and smells around her. She no longer needed to follow Milo to Jethro's place but chose to keep that secret a bit longer.

As they closed on it from above, Marissa spied the roof of the big barn and stopped. Milo turned, questioning. "Let's approach downwind," she said. Turning left they inscribed a wide arc around the clearing until they were on the downhill side of the property. She sniffed the air. "Dog?" she whispered, glancing at Milo.

"Big'un." He nodded. "Name of Rocky. Sleeps on the porch." He pointed to the small house. The door opened and Marissa immediately recognized the big man, older, grayer and a little beefier but no mistaking him. The huge dog appeared in the doorway and ambled over to the Scout. It lifted a leg, anointing the rear tire of the truck then followed Jethro into the barn. A few minutes later he emerged and climbed behind the wheel. On the second try, the truck coughed and sputtered to life. Rocky lumbered out of the barn, barking, as Jethro put the truck in gear. "C'mon!" she heard the old man holler over the roar of the engine. The dog hopped up to the passenger seat.

"Reckon he's headed up," Milo whispered.

"To your farm?" He nodded. "Can we get there ahead of him?" He nodded again, turned and loped into the woods with Marissa close behind. They arrived at the clearing a full minute before Jethro. Scouting the area, Marissa positioned them near the old garage where Gunderson was working on the Jeep. He stepped out of the building when he heard the old truck rattling up the hill, waving Jethro over. The old man pulled up in front of Gunderson and got out of the truck. Marissa and Milo crouched a dozen feet away.

They shook hands. "Miss Jenny come down. Said y'all needed parts fer the Jeep?"

"I think it might be beyond fixing, Jethro. The wires have been eaten by rodents, the tires are all flat, and that's just what I can see right now."

"Why's Miss Jenny need it runnin'? I c'n fetch 'n carry fer y'all." He gestured with his thumb toward the truck. "Been doin' it since 'fore Rocky was a seed in his pappy's pecker. I done somethin' wrong?"

Gunderson shook his head. "No. It seems that she wants to leave because of Milo." Milo's face reddened. Marissa put a hand on his arm.

"Milo?"

"I guess he's been skulking around down a swimming hole, spying on naked college girls."

Jethro broke into a booming laugh. "Mr. Robert, I reckon ev'ry boy on this mountain done the same. Hell, did it myself when I was a young'n. Even when I weren't so young."

"Jenny said he snuck into their camp at night and fondled one of them. I guess she was passed out drunk." Marissa, frowning, glanced over at Milo. His face was beet red and his hand was on his cheek.

"That ain't s'good." Jethro shook his head. "The boy c'n get in real trouble that way."

Gunderson nodded. "Jenny thinks taking him away from here is best. I don't see how though. It seems to me there are young girls everywhere we can go. The boy just needs to learn."

"Hope that's all," Jethro said. "I 'member his paw. Know'd him since he wus a pup, younger'n Milo. Back then even, he wus a mean sum'bitch. Just liked hurtin' folks." The old man stared off into the distance. "He wus 'bout Milo's age when his folks up'n disappeared. I come up t'visit Grady - that'd be Milo's granddad - 'n he 'n the missus was gone. Car, clothes, everything. Left Carl sittin' on the porch." Jethro walked over to the truck and leaned on it, scratching Rocky behind the ear.

"Where'd they go?" Jethro shrugged. "They never came back?" Jethro shook his head. Gunderson paced back and forth from the garage to the truck, shaking his head. "Carl stayed here all alone?"

"Yep. I come up time-t'-time t'see how he wus doin'. Hellova hunter that boy. Cain't 'member when they wadn't somethin' hangin' up bleedin'." They wadn't a better shot anywhere. That boy could take a grouse outta the air with a twenty-two." Admiration lit Jethro's face.

"When did Milo's mother show up?"

Jethro straightened. "Y'all mean his real maw or Miss Jenny?"

"His birth mother."

"That wus another strange thing. Carl, he went off to the war, Viet Nam, doncha-know. Come back drivin' that there Jeep." He nodded at the garage. "I'd hear him roll by 'bout ever evenin' first couple months, on his way t'town. Come back near dawn, he would, roarin' up the old road fit t'wake ev'ry critter in the woods." He frowned remembering. "Then come a time he stopped. Come down once, askin' t' use the forge for a day. Actually said, please. Didn't see no harm so I let'm but he wouldn't let me watch. Finished whatever it was late afternoon 'n left 'thout so much as a thank you. He stayed up on the mountain near four month 'fore showin' up again."

Marissa had hold of Milo's forearm; she was biting her lower lip, fighting to control her breathing. Milo put his hand over hers trying to pry it off his arm. She turned to him, looked at their hands, and released his arm, mouthing an apology. She turned her attention back to the two men. Jethro was speaking.

" ... 'n I said I could supply him with milk from my goats, long as it wan't too much. He said that'd be fine 'n left." He resumed scratching Rocky's ear. The dog groaned and leaned into Jethro's hand. "I milked next mornin' 'n drove on up. When I topped the rise I seen Carl standin' middle of the yard with his big ole arm 'round the prettiest young lady I mostly ever seen." The dog nearly fell out of the truck when Jethro pulled his hand away to point to where they were standing. "He said her name was Missy 'n they wus married 'n she wus gonna have a baby. Well I looked 'n seen she wus scared out of her mind." He shook his head. "I'da said somethin' but like I said, Carl wus a mean sum-bitch 'n that look in his eye gimme the creepin' willies, so I jus' nodded a hello 'n handed him the goat's milk 'n clumb in m'truck."

Marissa clenched and unclenched her fists. She glanced at Milo but his attention was riveted on the two men.

"So Missy is Milo's mother?"

"Yep. After Milo come, I'd see Missy in the yard with the babe 'n Carl seemed to be treatin' her real good. Din't see the same look in her eye, 'n they wasn't them switch-marks on her legs I usta see sometimes." He lumbered over to the Jeep, leaning heavily against the tailgate. "Didn't last, though. Milo wus near a year when I seen the marks agin 'n seen her eyes. Made me sad. Made me mad, too but, goddamn, that man scared me. Couldn't make myself do nothin'."

Marissa could see the old man's eyes tearing and deep down tried to forgive him.

"Went on near two year. Then one evenin' as I wus checkin' m' goats, Missy steps out of the woods. 'You gotta help me,' she says. I take one step, one damn step, 'n the sum-bitch appears right b'hind Missy, grabs her hair 'n runs his bowie knife 'crosst her neck 'n just throws her like she wan't more'n a doll, through the brush inta the woods. Then he looks at me 'n says. 'You seen nothin' old man. Haul ass back inside.' Jethro shook his head. Shames me t' say I done it."

Both men were silent. Marissa looked through her tears at Milo. He was kneeling, sitting on his heels, hands resting on his knees. With his left hand, he slowly reached for her neck. Marissa held her breath and remained still while his fingertips traced the long arc of the scar. When he withdrew his hand, she retrieved it with both of her own and placed it against her wet cheek. When Gunderson spoke they turned their attention back to the men.

"Then he got Jenny?" Jethro nodded.

"Yep, I'd hear his Jeep roarin' down the road in the evenin' then back 'fore daylight. Went on like that most nights, mebbe three - four months. One night he stops at m' house, bangin' the b'jesus out of the door till I open it. Well, he wants me t'come with him. Pickin' up a car, he says. Well I clumb in the Jeep 'n we head out like a red fox with 'r tail afire. We pull inta the lot by the Old Bull Inn down near the interstate. He pulls up next t' that Buick." He nodded to the red car deeper in the garage. He drives that'n back 'n I follow in the Jeep. Well we pull in, 'n he locks the place up 'n walks inta the house." Jethro smacked the flat of his hand hard on the tailgate of the Jeep. "I'm standin' there two mile from home on a cold damn night 'n the sum-bitch don't offer me a ride."

Gunderson nodded and patted the old man's shoulder. "That's Jenny's car. He didn't want anyone to find it and start looking for her."

"Sum-bitch," Jethro spat.

"What happened to Carl?"

Jethro stiffened and stepped away. "He's gone."

"I can see that, Jethro." Gunderson frowned and paced back and forth. *He's deciding whether to say something*, she thought and waited. "Jenny says … she says that she killed him." Marissa watched the old man's reaction. *And he's hiding something*, she thought.

"I reckon, it could be so."

"Jethro, I need to know."

160

The old man walked back to his truck. Rocky nuzzled Jethro's hand and was ignored. Finally, Jethro looked at Gunderson. "Miss Jenny, she's tough as an old steer. He beat on her jus' like he did Missy - I seen the marks - but she didn't never look as scared as Missy. Wus more like she wus waitin' fer somethin'."

"And she got it?"

Jethro nodded. "Mebbe ten year ago - 'bout that. She come outta the woods same as Missy, says, 'Jethro, I need your help.' Well, I'm so scared I'm 'bout to wet myself spectin' the sum-bitch t'come out 'n cut her neck like before, but he don't. 'I killed Carl', she says. So, I reckon that be your answer."

"What happened to his body?" Jethro's eyes danced side-to-side, looking everywhere but at Gunderson. He shrugged. *He knows*, Marissa thought.

"I'd best be goin'. You gonna want them parts?"

"I'm really not sure what all I need yet. Probably all the ignition stuff: wires, plugs, distributor parts." Gunderson shook his head. "Damn, Jethro. I really don't want to leave this place. I wish ... ah, hell. I wish I could convince Jenny." He shrugged. "I can't get her to sit still long enough to talk, what with her out hunting for Milo. I think we both know she won't find him unless he wants her to, but I can't convince her of that. I'd probably have to tie her to a chair or something."

At the door to his truck, Jethro turned. "I kinda like havin' y'all here. Miss Jenny seems ... happy, sorta." Jethro looked like he was pondering, trying to sort something out in his simple brain. His face lit up. "Want me t'find her fer ya?"

Gunderson hesitated, frowning. "Do you know where she might be?" Jethro nodded. "Sure. See if you can bring her back so we can talk about this some more." The old man climbed into the truck, cranked the engine

161

and hurried off with Rocky trying to steady himself in the seat.

Marissa nodded toward the game trail they'd come in on. Milo slipped into the brush with her at his heels. When they were back on the trail heading toward the cave, she touched his shoulder. Milo stopped, his back to her. "Milo?" He didn't move. She scooted around so she stood facing him and put her hands on his shoulders. He turned his face away. "Look at me, Milo." She touched his cheek, gently nudging his face toward hers, feeling the dampness on her fingertips. He let her do it, but his eyes focused on a point above her head, tears rolled down his cheeks. "Please, look at me."

Slowly his gaze lowered, taking in her features as if trying to memorize her. "You my maw?" She nodded. "You ain't daid?" She shook her head. She watched him process that information, watched him reach into his memory, watched him draw images out, and marked the pain contorting his face as he sorted them. Finally, Milo nodded once. "Paw wus mean."

Marissa turned and walked a few steps then came back. Hands clasped, index fingers steepled, she pointed in the general direction of Jethro's farm. "It was the day after your second birthday." She closed her eyes. "Your paw started beating me in the yard, I don't remember why … doesn't matter." Opening her eyes, she looked at Milo. "You were playing by the garden. When I screamed, you ran over to us. I remember you, so small and thin, pounding on his leg with your tiny fists. 'don't hurt mommy' you yelled. He smacked you so hard with the back of his hand … that he knocked you unconscious." She took a breath and continued. "I think it scared him. I think he thought he killed you. He stopped beating me and dragged me over to where you were lying and threw me down then walked into the barn." Marissa smiled at Milo. "Thank God, you were only stunned. I wrapped my arms around you. We sat there in the dirt rocking back and forth while you whimpered and a big red welt grew on your cheek." She shook her head. "You never howled, not like other kids. Just those quiet moans and sobs in a whisper. I knew then that I had to get you, us, away from him. That night, after he'd finished most of a jug of moonshine and was snoring like an old dog, I snuck out and ran, fast as I could down to Jethro's." She touched her scar. "You heard what happened next. I'm lucky. He was so damn drunk that he didn't hit anything vital." She paced up along the path and back several times. "I managed to crawl into Jethro's barn. I found an old shirt in there and pressed it on the wound. I don't know how long I was there. Finally I got up and started running down the coal road. The last thing I remember was hearing a diesel engine." Marissa stared hard at Milo. "For months, I couldn't remember my name. When I finally did, there was a block of years that were gone. Your years. It all came rushing back when I heard Jenny, your maw, say your father's name." She grabbed his shoulders. "I would never have left you on purpose. Please ... please believe me. I just couldn't remember." Milo nodded but Marissa couldn't read his expression. When she released his shoulders, he stepped around her and walked up the trail.

Chapter 16

That evening in the cave, after Marissa re-hydrated a pouch of soup, sharing it and three energy bars with Milo, they sat against opposite walls, lost in their separate, but connected memories. Milo shot glances in her direction from time to time. She decided that he'd talk when he was ready, finding her own solace in knowing he had survived ... in spite of her failure. She knew that she had Jenny to thank for that. She was thinking about Jenny and Gunderson, trying to sort out her next steps when she became aware of Milo's stare.

"Whut wus you b'fore you wus my ... my maw?"

Marissa smiled. She pulled her knees to her chest, resting her chin on her arms. "I was almost a biologist. Actually, I had a bachelor's degree in bio and was working on a master's." She stopped then, seeing the confusion on Milo's face. "You don't know what I'm talking about do you?" Milo shrugged. "You know about schools, right?"

"Maw teaches me." Marissa nodded.

"Okay. Well ... You know something about college, at least about college girls." Milo's blush made Marissa laugh out loud. "We'll talk more about that later," she said. "College is were people go to learn more things." She searched her brain for examples that he could relate to. "Your Maw, you said she was a nurse, right?" Milo nodded. "Well she had to learn a lot of things to become one, so she went to college to do that." She thought of another example, adding, "The books you learn from, they were written by people who learned a lot of things in college." His expression told her that he had a grasp of the concept.

"So, to get back to what I was saying, I was on a break, a vacation, from college when your father ... took me and brought me to the mountain." Marissa felt her heart rate increase. Closing her eyes for a moment, she worked to calm herself. When she opened them, Milo was looking at her with evident concern.

"I'm okay, Milo," she assured him. "Some of these memories are really hard." He nodded, relaxing a little. Marissa continued. "He never said it, but I'm sure he wanted to have a child, a boy to teach about all this." Her sweeping gesture took in their surroundings. "And here you are."

"Paw wus mean," Milo said, again. "He hurt you, terrible. Maw, too."

"Yes, he did." His faced reflected profound sadness. "But, the good thing that even his meanness couldn't destroy, was you." She rose, crossing the cave to sit beside him and took his hand in hers. "For all the bad he did, he taught you well. I am impressed with your skills." Marissa waited a long moment for him to make eye contact then added, hesitantly, "I am proud that you're my son."

Milo turned away, then back, worry clouding his face. "But my Maw ..."

"She did a wonderful job raising you, I can see that. But ..."

"I need t'talk to Maw." He stood, Marissa's hand still holding his. She used it to get to her feet and turn him to face her. "Gotta see Maw." He tried to free his hand but she held her grip.

"I know, Milo. We both need to talk to her, but let's wait just a little longer, please?"

"Whut fer?" He tugged again.

Marissa knew that if he got serious about freeing himself, she'd have to resort to violence to restrain him. She weighed her options. "Let me tell you about after I got out of the hospital and why I came here, then we'll talk

165

about seeing your Maw." She waited for him to relax then released her grip and motioned for him to sit. When he did, she sat between him and the mouth of the cave.

"It took a long time for me to get out of the hospital. That was because I didn't remember who I was. The FBI was there."

Milo nodded. "I heared, Paw yellin' at Maw onct 'bout FBI … never comin' or somethin'."

Marissa continued. "They told me my name and where I was from and where I disappeared from, but nothing was jogging my memory. Then one day a man in a wheelchair came in. His name is Harvey, an FBI psychologist. He worked with me using little bits about my past, he called them triggers, until I finally was able to actually remember my name, instead of just tell them I did. I remembered where I was from, my family, everything except the years I was missing. Harvey said we had no triggers for that time."

"But then y'heared Maw." Marissa nodded. She pulled a bar of dark chocolate from a pouch, broke it in half and handed one piece to Milo. He examined it then took a small bite, chewed it then shoved the rest in his mouth, grinning.

"When I got out, I went to visit Harvey at his office - to thank him. He started to tell me about a new program they were starting, training people to be expert trackers. They've lost people in the back country and, even with their technology they can't seem to find them so they decided to train people specifically to do that." Marissa smiled at the memory. "Anyway, I applied for it. My biology degree helped me because I could identify wildlife and plants pretty readily. I seemed to know a lot about actually tracking game also, like it came naturally to me." She frowned then. "I imagine some of your father's skills rubbed off when he had us out in the woods."

166

"So, yer a FBI'er?"

Marissa nodded. "A tracker. That's a special agent who finds people who are lost, or try to get lost."

"Why'd ya come here?" Milo's face showed concern. "Ya' takin' Maw away?"

"No, Milo. Why would I?"

"Paw done took her, like he took you."

Marissa nodded. "That's true, but nobody ever reported her missing. At least I don't know if they did. No, I'm actually here for Gunderson." Seeing his confusion, she added, "Mr. Robert."

"Whut'd he do?"

"He ran away from the FBI and they want him back."

Milo rose and Marissa tensed, but he went to the back of the cave to retrieve his bedroll. He lay down and wrapped himself in the furs. Resisting the urge to tuck him in, she prepared her own bed, angled so he'd have to step over her to leave the cave. Lying on her side, she listened until his even breathing told her he was asleep then she relaxed, allowing her own weariness to take over.

Chapter 17

The song of a Kentucky Warbler woke her just at dawn. The fire was already warming their shelter. *Damn he's good*, she thought proudly when she realized he was cooking another rabbit. She sat up, stretched and repacked her gear.

"Rabbit'l take a bit'a time, if y'all wanna go in back 'n hum agin."

Marissa laughed. "Guess I'll do just that," she said, rising and padding to the rear of the cave. She performed a short series of sun salutations. By the time she'd finished that, and her 'humming', Milo had the rabbit divided evenly and had added a stale biscuit to each serving.

They ate slowly, Marissa savoring the morning, with her son, Milo deep in his own thoughts. Finally she got down to business. "Does Mr. Robert ever leave the farm?" Milo turned his attention to her and shook his head.

"Does he stay in the house, with your Maw?"

"Uh uh. He sleeps in the tool shed. Fixed it up real nice, too." Engaged now, he added. "We wus gonna be buildin' a washin' place on the sun wall where we c'n clean game." His excitement faded. "Least ways we wus, 'til Maw begun talkin' 'bout leavin'. Ain't never gonna git'r done now." He tossed a small bone into the fire and spat some grizzle into it, causing a flash as the flame consumed it.

"Does he get up early?" Milo shook his head.

Marissa decided she needed another day of recon at least before moving in. "Milo, here's what we're going to do today. I want to go back to the farm and watch a while without Mr. Robert or Maw seeing us. We'll do that today and then tomorrow we'll go talk to your Maw without Mr. Robert knowing about it." She scanned his face, seeing puzzlement then a kind of resigned acceptance.

"I reckon," he said.

"Okay then. Let's get cracking." They spread the waning fire on the rock to cool and headed down the path toward the farm.

"Ma'am?" Milo said as they walked.

"Milo, you can call me Marissa if you want." She hesitated then added, "or Missy."

He nodded. "I wus just wonderin' what that was you was doin' in back, b'fore the hummin' that is."

Marissa chuckled. "It's called yoga. It helps me keep my body in shape. The humming is called chanting. It helps me ease my mind."

They walked on a little before Milo spoke again. "C'n y'all teach me the stretchin' 'n the hummin'?"

"I'd be happy to. We can start in the morning."

They arrived at the farm to see Gunderson and Jethro standing by the garage. From their position on the far side of the yard, Marissa couldn't hear the conversation but she saw Jethro gesture toward the barn, clearly heard Gunderson shout "You what?" then turn and run for the barn door. Jethro, head down, climbed into his truck and rode out of sight down the hill.

A few minutes later Jenny came racing out of the barn with Gunderson on her heels. Marissa lost sight of them when they reached the far side of the cabin and motioned for Milo to move. They skirted the edge of the woods to a point where they could see the porch, just as Jenny spun and slapped Gunderson hard.

"Was that just because I called him stupid?" He grabbed Jenny and continued. "What in hell is wrong?"

The argument seemed to be about Gunderson's relationship to Jethro. Marissa was mildly interested based on her experience with Jethro so she listened and watched while they argued.

"I swear, Jenny. I've never seen the place."

Jenny folded her arms across her chest. "Then how do you know Rocky?"

He grinned. "Jethro brought him up on the truck when he came to ask about parts for the cars."

Marissa saw that Jenny didn't believe him. She also noticed that Jenny backed off. *Smart move,* she thought. When the two separated, Jenny into the cabin and Gunderson to the tool shed, Marissa sat back to think. Her plan was to meet the woman tomorrow and she didn't like to deviate from a plan unless it was necessary. The opportunity seemed to be presenting itself but she wasn't sure she was ready for the contact. What does one say to the woman who raised your child? Whatever it is, tomorrow is time enough.

Milo tapped her on the shoulder. Pointing up the mountain, he turned and disappeared into the woods. Marissa followed.

Chapter 18

Back at the cave Marissa volunteered some of her freeze-dried supplies as input to a stew. Milo retrieved a cast iron pot while she made a small fire. They combined the ingredients with water, heated it up and ate with the pot between them. They dipped into the stew with small hollowed gourds, not speaking, immersed in their thoughts.

Shortly after dark, Milo hauled his bedroll out and curled into it. Marissa spread her bedding and stretched out, hands behind her head. Milo's deep breathing told her he was asleep. She envied his ability to reach that state so easily. Her mind raced, pulling her back to a past that, with one exception, she wanted to forget - had forgotten until now.

At dawn the following morning, Marissa and Milo made their way down the game trail to the farm. When they were close, they veered away from the cabin, instead approaching the tool shed. Marissa listened at the back wall until she was certain she heard Gunderson's regular breathing then they circled the clearing, stopping in the trees fifty feet from the cabin door.

"Milo, we're going to go talk to your maw now." He rose, but she put a hand on his arm. I don't want your maw to know I'm an FBI agent, you remember that, right?" Milo nodded. "Okay, let's go."

When they reached the door, Milo opened it and stepped in. Marissa followed a few steps behind.

***

Staring out the window at the closed door of the tool shed, Jenny mixed the sourdough batter with more vigor than usual. The large wooden spoon clattered against the bowl in the crook of her arm like the clapper in a muffled bell. Her anger at Robert vied for prominence with her fear of losing Milo. At the sound of the door, she turned to see Milo step into the room. The bowl slipped from her arm and she dropped the spoon to catch it. She hurried to Milo, setting the bowl on the table to free her hands, and wrapped him in her arms, tears streaming down her cheeks. "Milo, Milo, Milo." She stepped back putting her hands on his shoulders to get a better look at him and saw a woman standing in the threshold. "Who …?"

"Maw, this here's Missy. She be m' maw … too."

The woman stepped forward looking a little exasperated and extended her hand. Eyes locked on the woman, Jenny backed up until she hit the table. She used both hands to steady herself while her foot dragged a chair out, then she sat.

"I think we have a lot to talk about. May I sit?" the woman asked. Jenny nodded. Milo shifted his weight from one foot to the other, tried to find a place for his hands then scooted up the loft ladder and disappeared over the edge.

Jenny stared, not blinking, not speaking, not moving; her eyes never left Marissa's face.

"My name's Marissa Landry. Sixteen years ago, Carl Larson kidnapped me and brought me here," she said, stretching her arms out to the side, palms up. "He …" She glanced at the loft. "He brought me here to give him a child, a male child. I'm pretty sure I'd be dead if Milo …" She glanced at the loft again.

"I'm sure you're right," Jenny finally said. "There's no need to continue."

"I think I have to."

Jenny sighed. "Milo, get down here, boy." Milo was at her side before she'd completed the sentence. "You check your snares lately?"

He looked from her to Marissa and back. "I reckon not."

"Be back by high sun," she said. Milo left through the still-open door. Both women watched him fade into the woods. "Close the door." Marissa rose to obey. "And lock it," Jenny added.

When Marissa returned, she said, "Before I continue, I told you who I am. You are?"

"The woman who's listening to you. Now, you wanted to keep going so go ahead. You can skip the details about being raped and beaten, I've been there. How in hell did you get away from the bastard?"

Jenny listened as Marissa retold the story of her lucky escape, her amnesia, and living with three years missing from her life until forty-eight hours ago. When she finished, Jenny's eyes narrowed. "Okay, so you didn't remember any of this until you were here. Why are you up on the mountain then? There aren't any hiking trails within thirty miles in any direction."

"I'm a plant biologist. I heard rumors that there was a stand of *Abies balsamea,* Balsam Fir, somewhere up in these mountains. They're fairly rare around West Virginia."

Jenny nodded. "So, this was just a coincidence, you showing up here?"

Marissa shrugged. "I don't know. Maybe something down deep in my unconscious pushed me here. Maybe I needed to get those years back."

Jenny stood and walked over to the sink then turned to face Marissa. "How about cutting the bullshit? You're way too self-assured, way too in control to be a field biologist meeting up with a son you didn't remember in a place you didn't remember." She pointed to Marissa's utility belt. "Besides, I don't believe a field biologist would

173

carry a Marine's K-bar knife. What in hell are you, Marissa? If that's even your name."

Marissa's brow furrowed. Jenny stared at her and she at Jenny; neither moved for more than a minute then Marissa spoke. "My name is Marissa Landry. I am Milo's biological mother; you can verify that with Jethro. I am also in fact a biologist by education, though that's not what I do for a living." Marissa stood and retrieved her badge. "I am an FBI agent, an expert tracker, and I came here to retrieve a fugitive."

Jenny's legs started to buckle and she gripped the sink for support. She gasped, trying to find her breath with little success and would have sunk to the floor had not Marissa guided her to the nearest chair. "It's over," she moaned.

"Ms. Benedict? Does Gunderson mean that much to you?"

Jenny shook her head to clear it. "You ... Robert?"

"Lars Robert Gunderson. He escaped from FBI custody a few months ago. I came here to bring him back."

"How ...?"

"The savings account in his name at a bank in Luray, Virginia. I followed Jethro back to the coal road when he made the July deposit, though I didn't recognize him then." Marissa crouched in front of Jenny. "I assume you are Jennifer Benedict."

Hearing the full name after so many years made Jenny shiver. "Yes. Yes, I am."

Marissa sat in the chair opposite Jennifer Benedict and waited for her to compose herself. When her breathing had slowed and her face had gained some color, Marissa continued. "I met Milo by accident in the woods behind the old garage. That was where I overheard Gunderson and you talking. Milo was listening too, though I didn't know that until later." She watched Jenny's reaction to the news that Milo had been there before continuing with the exchange between Gunderson and Jethro.

Jenny straightened when she heard that conversation, saying simply, "Ah, I understand."

Marissa let that pass. "I have to take Gunderson back." Jenny nodded. "I'd like to come back to visit Milo when I'm done with him. Are you okay with that?" Jenny nodded.

Marissa walked to the door. As she reached for the latch, Jenny said, "You can't have him."

Marissa turned. "Excuse me?"

"I won't let you take him."

"I'm afraid I have to Ms. Benedict. Gunderson is wanted by the FBI." She unlocked the door. "Please don't try to interfere." Jenny nodded. "Promise me I won't have any trouble with you now."

"Where's Milo?"

"You sent him out to …"

"Rat here, Maw," Milo answered from his perch on the porch step.

Marissa walked over to the step and sat beside him. "I have to go Milo, but I'll be back to see you soon."

"Ah'd like that."

"You can't have Milo," said Jenny from the doorway.

"I know," said Marissa. She rose and walked toward the tool shed.

Milo's Gift

Chapter 19

Marissa handed Gunderson over to agents Sharp and Carson in the parking garage then took the elevator up to the third floor and hurried to Harvey's office to give him the news. She stopped at his closed door, hesitated a moment then knocked.

"Yeah?"

"It's Marissa, you busy?"

"Always. Door's not locked. Come on in." Harvey was on the phone when she entered. He waved her to a chair. "Okay Archie, thanks," he said. Dropping the phone on its cradle, he rolled his chair back and turned to face her. "You've got that Cheshire cat grin Missy, talk."

She slid to the edge of the chair. "I got my three years back, Harvey!" she announced, reaching out for him.

Delancey rolled close and held her hands. Marissa tried to keep still while he scrutinized her face, but she found it impossible not to fidget. She knew him well enough not to say anything until he responded to her announcement. After a seemingly endless silence, he released her hands and sat straight in his chair. "I'm listening."

She started with the dreams and the flashes of recognition in areas around the mountain where she found Gunderson. When she got to the conversation between Jenny and Gunderson that brought everything back, her voice rose in pitch. She breathed in short gasps, her recollections firming up in the telling. She was oblivious to Delancey's movements when he rolled over to close his office door then pulled his chair close beside her seat, unaware that she rose and paced the room while she spoke, unaware that tears ran down her cheeks as each detail of those years materialized, unaware that she had curled into a fetal position on his sofa after an hour, drained of everything but weariness.

She woke covered with an olive-drab wool blanket, the sky outside the window was dark, and Harvey Delancey was working at his desk, with the green-shaded desk lamp his only light. He glanced over at the sound of her movement.

"How you doing?"

Marissa slid the blanket off and sat, flexing her back muscles and stretching her arms over her head. "Guess I was tired," she said through a yawn. "I'm okay, old man."

Delancey turned his chair to face her. "Missy Mae, I'm going to hook you up with the psych department for a couple of days."

"Ah dammit, Harvey. I got this. I'm okay now."

"Maybe. Maybe you are, but I want them to tell me that."

"Come on. Please?" Marissa stood, arms folded. "You're a shrink, Harvey. You just heard everything. Why can't you tell me?"

"Missy, I'm too close. I care about you. I need an impartial eval." He handed her a sealed envelope. "Take this to Psych in the morning. Now get your butt out of my office."

She took the envelope, yanked the door open and slammed it on her way out.

Chapter 20

The following morning a grumpy Marissa Landry presented herself at the second floor offices of the Testing and Evaluation Department. "I'm supposed to see Dr. ..." she checked the name on the envelope. "Belden."

The young lady behind the reception desk, whose name, according to the ID badge hanging around her neck, was Alexa Lockwood, smiled briefly. "Have a seat," she said. Reaching for the phone, she punched a button. "Your eight-thirty is here." Still standing at the desk, Marissa held out the envelope. "You should give that to the doctor, Ms. Landry."

On her way to the nearest chair she heard, "Marissa Landry?" and turned to see a tall slender woman in black jeans and blouse, with long hair the same color. Her angular face was tanned, as were her hands. The hem of her jeans hid black cowboy boots. Marissa approached and held out the envelope. The woman took it then extended her hand. "I'm Erin Belden."

Marissa shook her hand. "Can't say I'm pleased to meet you." The doctor smiled.

"Come in and let's talk. I'll try to make this as painless as possible."

Marissa looked at the two identical chairs facing each other at a slight angle. The only difference was the coffee cup resting on the small table beside the one on the left. She sat in that chair. With no hesitation, Dr. Belden took the other. "Excuse me just a moment," she said. She tapped one end of the long envelope on the arm of the chair, tore off the other, blew into the open end and withdrew a single sheet, handwritten, Marissa noticed by the light over the doctor's shoulder. She chuckled then folded the note up and returned it to the envelope, tossing it onto the nearby desk.

"May I call you Marissa?" Marissa nodded. "Okay, Marissa. Dr. Delancey indicates that you've been hit with an almost instant recollection of three horrible years in captivity. Is that about right?" Marissa nodded. "Tell me about it please." Marissa looked around the office trying to decide how much to tell and how much to leave out.

"Marissa, I had quite a long phone conversation with Dr. Delancey yesterday afternoon, during which he related what you told him, so I know the details. I'd like to hear them from you." Dr. Belden rose and retrieved her coffee cup, placing it on the table beside her chair. "The sooner we start, the sooner we're finished."

Marissa retold the story with the same level of detail she had related to Harvey, but was able to maintain her composure throughout the telling. When she finished, she was perspiring and felt like she could fall asleep in a heartbeat, but she was in control.

"Marissa, I want you to close your eyes and take us back to the smokehouse."

"What? I already told you. He hung me up by my arms and beat me."

"You did a great job of reporting it, but you weren't there. Let's go there."

"What are you? Some kind of freaking voyeur?" Marissa felt her pulse quicken. "That's in the past. Carl Larson is gone. The monster is dead."

"Is he?"

"Of course he is! I spoke to the person who killed him."

"Did you see the body?"

"No! It was ten years ago!" She fought for control.

"Then you can't be sure, can you?"

180

"He can't be alive! Jenny said." Marissa was shaking.

"What if she was wrong?"

Marissa pulled her knees to her chest and rocked back in the chair. "He's dead," she sobbed. "He's dead."

"Not to you, Marissa. He's still alive in you, Marissa." The doctor placed her hand on Marissa's right arm. She said, "Go to the smokehouse. Be in the smokehouse." Marissa closed her eyes. She pushed her mind back until she could feel the tightness of the leather on her wrists, the strain on her shoulder sockets, her feet dangling inches above the dirt floor. She could smell the smoked meat and blood, feel the sting of the switch on her back and legs, of her own sweat in her wounds. She heard a scream and realized it was her. Dr. Belden's voice pulled her back slowly. Finally her breathing slowed and she sagged in the chair. "Marissa, relax, if you can." Marissa obeyed. They were silent for several minutes.

"I'll see you same time tomorrow," the doctor said, finally. Walking to the door as she spoke, she opened it and waited. "Go home and rest." She let Marissa out.

Chapter 21

The following morning, Marissa approached the office with great trepidation. "Go right in," Alexa said when she reached the reception desk. She veered off, making for Erin Belden's open office door.

The doctor was seated in the same chair as yesterday, coffee cup beside her. She was dressed in black again, turtleneck shirt the only difference.

"Good morning, Marissa." She sipped her coffee while Marissa took her seat. "How did you sleep?"

She frowned. "Is that a clinical or a social question, doc?"

The doctor shrugged. "Take your pick."

"I slept like shit." The doctor nodded.

"Today, I want you to take me to Milo's cave."

Marissa straightened. "Okay."

"Close your eyes and tell me again about your days in the cave."

Dr. Belden leaned forward, focused on Marissa's face. She closed her eyes and went back to the days in the cave, her pride in Milo's prowess in the woods, the way he maintained his lair. Her smile broadened when she spoke about his interest in the *hummin' n stretchin'*. She felt the doctor's hand on her left arm. "How did you feel when he asked?"

"Fantastic! He's such a great kid!" Marissa answered.

The gentle strokes on her left arm stopped suddenly, replaced by a hand on her right arm. Her pulse quickened and she could feel the smokehouse coming back. Before she succumbed to the panic, the hand was gone, replaced by a touch on her left arm. Her pulse slowed as a vision of Milo, walking ahead of her on the trail materialized. The touch was suddenly on the right arm, then the left, right, left, right, left, each pass a shorter duration until, finally both arms were touched at the same time. Marissa stiffened as if a jolt of electricity were passing through her; images of the smokehouse and Milo flashed in and out until neither existed as an entity. She gasped for air, realizing she'd been holding her breath.

"Okay, Marissa. Open your eyes." Dr. Belden was on her knees, a hand on each of Marissa's arms. She let Marissa go and returned to her own seat.

"What just happened?"

"We took two emotional extremes and kind of morphed them into a third, less intense sensation. The technical term is collapsing anchors." The doctor shook her head. "Among ourselves we call it magic. I don't know why it works, but it does."

"So that means … means what?"

"Basically, that your Carl Larson obsession won't bother you anymore, not even if you're standing inside that smokehouse with him." Marissa noted no flash of panic at his name or the image. The doctor continued, "The downside is that the intense joy and pleasure you felt around that incident with Milo, is gone also. You'll remember it, just like you remember the smokehouse, but the emotional intensity is gone."

Marissa sighed. "Collateral damage?" Belden nodded.

The doctor rose and offered Marissa her hand, which she gratefully accepted. At the office door, she turned. "Dr. Belden?"

"Yes?"

"What did Harvey say in that note?"

183

"His words were, 'She's in worse shape than she knows. She's special. Help her.'"

"What part of that made you chuckle?" Marissa asked, a little testily.

"There was a post script. It said, 'Missy Mae is a brilliant girl, Erin. Don't let her con you.'" The doctor met her at the door. "Did you?" Marissa shook her head and left.

Chapter 22

The following Monday, Marissa entered Delancey's office and sat on the leather sofa waiting for him to get off the phone.

"How're you feeling, Missy Mae?" he said, after he hung up.

"Every time you ask me that. I end up talking with a shrink."

He laughed. "Not this time." He picked up a folder and held it out to her. "I'm going to file this with Gunderson's records, not that we need it anymore." She got up and took it, dropping into the chair next to his desk to read. It was a dossier on Jennifer Benedict. She flipped through the file, giving each sheet a quick scan before returning to the first page. The photo stapled to the upper left corner was an ID shot of her in an army nurses' uniform. Benedict had been commissioned in 'sixty-seven, served a double tour in China Beach where she was injured in a mortar attack, spent seven months at Bethesda Naval Hospital before being transferred to Fort Belvoir Hospital in Virginia for physical therapy, and finally discharged with a permanent disability in nineteen seventy-two.

Marissa flipped to the third page, verified that disability payments were deposited directly to her account at *Luray Savings and Loan* then went back to the first sheet.

Her injury had been a shattered hip from being thrown into a wall by the concussion from a mortar round. The damage was great enough to warrant several surgeries and finally the medical discharge. She flipped back and forth among the pages several times then closed the folder. "Can I hang on to this for a few days?"

"Don't see why not. Drop it off here when you're done."

"Will do." She tucked the folder under her arm, stood and walked to the door. "Dinner tonight?" she asked at the threshold.

"Sure. Where?"

"You pick." She heard him laughing as she closed the door.

Chapter 23

Harvey called an hour after Marissa reached her apartment. "Italian?"

"You said there was a new Thai restaurant in town," she said. "How about that?"

"Good to know you haven't changed," he said. "Pick you up at seven?"

"Make it seven-thirty." She hung up and returned to the dossier, studying the last page for the forth time. She couldn't shake the feeling that something was wrong. Somewhere in these dozen pages was a disconnect, an anomaly; she felt it and long ago learned to trust her gut. "Damn!" She slammed the folder down on her coffee table, rose and paced the room. Nothing in the documents was out of whack, nothing. "What is it?" She went to the kitchenette, pulled a twelve-ounce tumbler from a shelf above the sink and filled it from the tap.

Brow furrowed, Marissa stepped back from the sink, reaching behind with her free hand to locate the small kitchen table. When her fingertips found the smooth maple edge, she leaned against it then snapped upright, eyes wide. She set the tumbler down hard on the counter then rushed to the coffee table and grabbed the file. She opened to the front page, to Captain Jennifer Benedict's description and pointed to it. She read it aloud. "*Height: 5' 7"*, same as me." The woman up on the mountain was at least two inches taller. She closed the folder, shoved it under her arm and left the apartment.

Chapter 24

Marissa rapped on the ornate front door of Delancey's small brick house. "Wasn't I supposed to pick you up at seven-thirty?" he said when he saw her standing on his porch, still in jeans and T-shirt. "And the Thai place is a little classier than biker chick."

"The woman on the mountain isn't Jenny Benedict."

"Come on in, girl." He rolled his chair back to let her pass.

She hurried into Delancey's living room and sat on the sofa. She opened the folder when he reached the end of the coffee table. Handing the first page over, she said, "Jennifer Benedict and I are the same height. The woman on the mountain is about two inches taller. Harv, people don't grow taller between twenty-two and forty."

"Her height could have been mistyped or even intentionally wrong. I knew a guy, drafted into the army, about twenty pounds over the max weight for his height. The doc added two inches on the chart and accepted him." He handed the sheet back. "The anomaly is interesting, but by itself, it doesn't mean much."

"I think it's worth looking into a little deeper. What happened to her after she left Belvoir? Did she stay with relatives? Her address on the DD-214 is a PO Box in Timberville. Why bank in Luray?" Marissa gestured with the folder as she spoke. "Too many questions, Harv." She dropped the folder on the coffee table and leaned forward. "Besides, that's my son up there with a person who isn't who she claims to be." Arms resting on her knees, she turned her hands palm upward and waited, as if expecting a load of wood.

"Okay, Missy Mae, I'm convinced." Delancey leaned forward, picked up the folder and deposited it in her arms. "You have a new assignment." He backed up and spun the chair around to face the front door. "Now get your butt home and pretty up so you don't embarrass me at dinner." He held the door open for her.

Chapter 25

Two days later Marissa drove through the main gate at Fort Belvoir. Through Harvey, she'd gotten permission from DOD to look through Jennifer Benedict's records. Inside, she asked at the information desk for the records center and was directed to a bank of elevators down a long hall to the right. She rode the staff elevator down to the lower level and saw the door marked *Records* directly across the narrow hall. Behind the wire-reinforced glass in the door, sat a corporal in fatigues, feet propped on his desk, perusing the latest issue of *Hustler*. As soon as Marissa keyed the intercom his feet hit the floor and the magazine disappeared under the blotter. "Yes?" he said, standing to look through the window.

"Special Agent Marissa Landry, FBI. I believe you're expecting me." When she heard the click of the electric lock, she pushed open the door and walked in. "I need all you have on this person." She handed him a card with Benedict's Army serial number and social security number. Reciting the serial number under his breath, the young man dropped the card on his desk and hurried down a row of shelves. Half a minute later he reappeared with a large envelope about three inches thick and handed it to her.

"You can sit over at one of them tables over there." He pointed to a place behind her. "You ain't supposed to take anything out of here." Marissa nodded.

She sat at the closest table, unwound the string closure, slid the contents out and sorted them into separate piles: medical procedures, psychological evaluations, therapy records, and other. The most recent items in the three major piles told her that the hip injury would likely cause severe arthritis later in life, that she had responded well to therapy and was walking without aid, but with a serious limp that was likely permanent, and that she was suffering from mild depression and should continue therapy on an outpatient basis. The small 'other' pile contained copies of her discharge papers indicating permanent disability, and several other records of no interest to Marissa. One sheet stood out. It was a recommendation that Jennifer be provided with a full-time nurse at her residence for the first six months following her discharge, with a reevaluation after that period to determine if there was continued need. Six names followed in alphabetical order with addresses and phone numbers. Marissa glanced over to the desk. The corporal had his feet on the desk again, a manila folder open in front of his face. She quietly folded the sheet and slipped it into her pocket then returned the rest of the material to the envelope.

"I'm finished now," she said, dropping the envelope on the desk. "Thanks." She opened the door.

The young man peered over his hidden *Hustler* magazine. "Sure."

Marissa left Fort Belvoir, driving south on US 1 toward Quantico. After booking a room at the Visitor's Quarters for the weekend, she unfolded the list, faxed it to Harvey before adding it to the dossier then changed and went out for a long run. Three hours later she sat on the bed in a full lotus, dialing the first number on the list.

Chapter 26

"Four of the numbers belonged to people who never knew the women I have listed for them, the other two don't remember being contacted back then by Benedict or the army," Marissa told Delancey over the phone the next morning.

"Interesting, girl, but couldn't it have waited until Monday? I have a life outside work you know."

"Then why am I talking to you on your office phone?"

"Don't be a smart-ass. Hang on." She kept the phone to her ear, hearing muffled voices then he came back on the line. "Three of your list are accounted for …" she heard papers rustling. "Hear they are: Bridie Hanes and Mildred Murphy have no recollection of Benedict, Claire Kry … Kryznyski, I think – damn Poles – is deceased. We're working on the other three. Hang on." Muffled voices again then he was back. "That's it for now. Don't bother me until Monday."

"Wait! Before you hang up you old fart, get photos of all the women on the list, if you can. Even the dead ones … especially them." She hung up the phone.

***

Saturday afternoon Marissa worked out with one of the martial arts instructors at the FBI training center. That evening and most of Sunday she pored through the library, devouring everything she could on the geography of southern West Virginia. Monday morning she packed the van and drove to Richmond, arriving shortly before ten. Delancey's third floor office was dark. Grumbling, she turned and almost ran into agent Sharp. "Whoa, sorry, Sharp."

"It's okay, ma'am. You were looking for the director?" Marissa nodded. "He called in sick this morning."

"Thanks," Marissa said hurrying to the elevator.

She parked in Delancey's driveway behind his car and walked to the door. It opened before she could ring the bell. "I heard you roar up, Missy Mae. That machine is government property so you damn well better take care of it," Delancey growled. "Now, what are you doing here?" He backed up to let her in.

"Sharp told me you called in sick," she said, not entering. "You're such an old geezer, I got worried."

"Mental health day, girl. You should try it sometime. By the way, I think they have your photos at the shop."

"I wish somebody had told me that when I was there."

"Agent Sharp called while you were abusing your van on the way over here. She had the photos, but you hightailed it out before she could hand them to you." He waved her toward the van. "Now get the hell out of here and give me some peace."

"Okay, okay. Pardon me for worrying." As she walked to the vehicle, Marissa called over her shoulder. "Nice PJ's! The polka-dots are really you." He was still laughing when she started the van.

When the elevator door opened at the third floor, Agent Sharp thrust a manila envelope toward Marissa with both hands and a big smile. She stepped into the hallway. Taking the envelope from the agent's hands, she grinned. "Don't say a word, Sharp."

"Not a syllable, ma'am."

She went into Delancey's office and flopped on the leather sofa, feet on the coffee table. The envelope had photos of five of the six women on the list. The photo of Claire Kryzynski was a young Jennifer Benedict. She smiled. "Gotcha."

A rap on the open door got her attention. Agent Sharp stepped in. "Thought you'd want these also," she said, dropping several folders on the coffee table. Marissa thanked her then fished through them until she came to Kryzynski. She sat back on the sofa and opened the file. Kryzynski's height was listed as 5' 91/2" and she was thirty-six, or would have been. According to the death certificate she expired in 1973. Cause of death: asphyxiation. She had died in a house fire in Timberville, VA. Investigators determined the cause to be an explosion due to a gas leak in the kitchen.

Marissa flipped the page and saw copies of two news clippings, an obituary for Claire Kryzynski, and a report on the fire stating that her employer, Jennifer Benedict was in the opposite end of the house when the explosion occurred and escaped with minor cuts and bruises. She put the photo in the file and closed it. "Okay Claire, are you a murderer or are you just defrauding the government?" She let out a sigh. "Let's find out." Springing to her feet she snatched the folder and hurried through the door to the elevator.

Chapter 27

Marissa arrived in Timberville shortly after three. After a quick stop at the Shell station for fuel and directions, she parked in front of the *Timberville Public Library* and walked in. The elderly woman behind the circulation desk smiled as Marissa approached. The name plate on her desk read *Harriet Maines*. "Do you have back issues of the local newspapers, Ms. Maines?"

"Why yes, dear. All the way back to 1897." She folded her hands in her lap. "What year are you interested in?"

"Nineteen seventy-three and seventy-four."

The librarian rose. "Those are all on film." She walked around the desk, motioning for Marissa to follow. "Come, I'll show you." They entered a small room at the far end of the library. Two desks faced each other in the center of the room, each topped with a large microfilm reader. The walls were lined with microfilm file cabinets. Harriet Maines led her to a cabinet in the far left corner of the room. "These are from seventy-two to seventy-eight," the librarian said, sweeping her hand from the top drawer down to the fifth. "Are you looking for anything in particular?" she asked, stepping aside. "I know it's not any of my business, so of course you needn't answer."

Displaying her ID, Marissa answered, "I'm trying to locate someone who disappeared in the early seventies." She returned the woman's smile.

The librarian nodded. "Oh my, an FBI agent. Well, dear. I've been librarian here for thirty-five years. I know almost everyone in town. Perhaps I can help."

"Oh that would be wonderful. Her name is Jennifer Benedict, a former Army nurse." Marissa held back from revealing her reasons. "I believe she settled here."

"Hm … Benedict. In the seventies you say?"

"Nineteen seventy-three, I believe."

"And she was in the Army?"

"Not when she moved here. She was injured pretty badly in Vietnam. She probably walked with a limp." Marissa withdrew the photo of Claire she'd pulled from her file. "This is the only picture I have of her." She handed the photo to the woman, who studied it for several seconds, cocking her head to one side then the other and back. Then her eyes widened.

"Oh, my! Of course! Terrible thing." The librarian opened the second of the five drawers, taking out a boxed microfilm roll labeled *July 1973*. She sat in front of the nearest reader, turned it on, and loaded the film. She spun the wheel, stopping every few seconds to check the date, slowing finally as she neared the day she was looking for. The machine stopped at the front page of the *Timberville Miller* dated July 23, 1973. "Here it is." She pointed to the headline, standing so Marissa could take the seat. The headline read, *EXPLOSION LEVELS HOME – NURSE KILLED!*

The details pretty much paralleled the clipping she had from the Harrisonburg paper, but this one had a photo of Claire – Jenny, clothing torn and blood streaming from a scalp wound. According to the reporter she was just leaving the house and had opened the front door when the explosion occurred. *The home's owner, Jennifer Benedict, was catapulted through the open door, landing in the seven-foot tall privet hedge that separated the house from state route 617. Debris fell all around her and on the hedge, but miraculously none hit her directly. The Timberville volunteer fire department responded quickly but the building was totally destroyed. The body of Miss Benedict's nurse was burned beyond recognition. Her name is being withheld pending notification of next-of-kin.* "Do you know what happened to Miss Benedict?" Marissa asked.

"As I recall, she got a fairly large settlement from the gas company and folks said she moved someplace around Harrisonburg."

"Did they ever find the nurse's next of kin?"

"Why, I don't know." She walked to the open file drawer. "We can look."

'No, thank you anyway. I really am more interested in Miss Benedict."

"Okay, dear." The librarian looked disappointed. Marissa thanked her again and headed for the door. Her next stop, the county courthouse. An hour of research there yielded the fact that Jennifer Benedict had accepted ninety-five thousand dollars as a settlement from the propane supplier. Her lawyer received thirty-two five, another thirty-two five was deposited in a blind trust in the name of Mildred Kryzynski of Lubbock, Texas, and the rest Jennifer Benedict took in the form of a certified check. Her address was the same PO box in Timberville as on her discharge papers.

Marissa drove south to Harrisonburg, booked a room at the Hampton Inn then found a small Italian restaurant for dinner. Back in her room she opened the file and grabbed a sheet of Hampton Inn stationary and a pen. She needed to get her thoughts out where she could see them. She started with *Claire = Jenny July seventy-three, must have stayed around Timberville until settlement* – she checked her notes from the courthouse – *May seventy-four, might have left right away for Harrisonburg.* She listed a series of questions: *Thirty thousand = car + bank deposit? When Luray? Why Luray? When me? Mildred Kryzynski?*

The following morning she called Delancey to bring him up to date.

"Okay, Missy. I'll see what we can dig up on Mildred. What about the lawyer?"

"What about him?"

"I'd bet he was in contact with our Jenny after the settlement, at least for a short time. Maybe he has a more recent address."

"Good point. I'll get on it."

"No, you keep doing your thing out there. Sharp and Carson will handle it."

"Okay." She hung up, grabbed the file and left.

At the Harrisonburg Police Department, her badge got her access to the chief, a sixtyish balding man whose belly hung over his black gun-belt, and who barely glanced at her badge and ID. "Can't say you look much like an FBI agent."

Standing in front of his desk, she resisted verbalizing the several responses that danced in her head. "I'm working undercover," she said.

"In Harrisonburg?" He leaned forward, his face reddening.

"No, not here." He relaxed a little. "I'm actually looking for a woman who may have come to Harrisonburg briefly in May of seventy-four."

"What're you, on cold cases?"

"Not exactly. This is an active investigation that I'm working up some background on. Her name is Jennifer Benedict." She waited.

The chief leaned forward again, hands clasped and resting on his desk. "What do you expect me to do with that?"

"I thought you might have somebody check your records to see if she was reported missing."

"A missing person from seventy-four? You're kiddin' right?"

Marissa saw that she was wasting her time. "I suppose so," she said, turning toward the door. As she opened it, she said over her shoulder, "Thanks for all your help."

She sat in the van for a few minutes before driving to the county sheriff's office. The results were pretty much the same, though more cordial. Frustrated, she drove back to Timberville, and the librarian.

Harriet Maines seemed genuinely happy to see Marissa. "I have something you might be interested in. It's about Jennifer Benedict."

"I'm definitely interested," she said, sitting in a straight-backed chair beside the desk.

"Well, I went through a few more weeks of the *Miller* and I found the nurse's name. It was Claire Kryzynski." She produced a sheaf of papers from her top drawer. "It seems, she had a sister in Texas somewhere, but they didn't find out until the nurse was buried. That caused a bit of a row, but Miss Benedict talked to her on the phone and she seemed to accept that she wasn't able to claim the body, or attend the funeral for that matter."

More than a little surprised, Marissa said, "All of that was in the news?"

The librarian chuckled, "Mercy no! I remembered that Sarah Hanes knew Miss Benedict, so I went over to her house for tea and a chat. She told me about the phone call."

Marissa perked up. "I wonder if Miss Hanes would mind speaking with me?"

"I think she'd be glad to. She doesn't get much company anymore." She picked up the phone. "I'll call and ask her right now."

Sarah Hanes greeted them at the door of her large Victorian home a few hundred feet from the place where Jennifer Benedict's once stood. She was stooped from osteoporosis and walked with the help of an ornately carved sassafras cane. "My lord, Harriet, didn't you get enough of my chatter yesterday?" The old woman opened the door wide. "Come in, come in. I'll put up tea." Leaving Marissa and the librarian in the foyer, she hurried down a long hall, disappearing through the open door at its end.

"She'll expect to see us in the parlor," the librarian said, entering the room on their left.

Marissa sat in a wingback chair opposite a massive marble-framed fireplace. With all the Victorian furniture, heavy upholstered sofas framed by ornate dark-stained wood bracketed a large oval coffee table, with several side chairs scattered around the walls of the large room, it felt like a chamber quartet could appear at any moment. Miss Maines perched on the edge of one of the sofas, smiling vacantly at Marissa. Sarah Hanes returned with a silver tray containing a teapot visible under a quilted cozy, three delicate-looking cups with matching saucers, and a plate of scones. Miss Maines introduced Marissa.

"My, my Miss Landry, an FBI agent and so young!" Marissa smiled.

She waited while the woman poured tea and offered the scones. Marissa took one then spoke. "Mrs. Hanes, I ..."

"Please, call me Sarah," the woman said. Taking a seat on the sofa opposite the librarian, she smoothed her dress then picked up her tea.

Marissa noticed the tremor in the old woman's hand as she brought the cup to her lips. "Sarah, I'm looking for anything that might help me find Jennifer Benedict." She glanced at the librarian then continued. "I'm sure you know how much I've discovered so far, with Miss Maines' help."

"Harriet told me, yes," she answered.

Marissa waited while the woman sipped her tea. "Did Miss Benedict visit you often?"

"At least once a week." Sarah Hanes gazed out the window in the direction of the absent house. "She'd come by for tea. Often we'd sit on the patio and watch the sunset."

"Did her nurse come with her?"

"Sometimes…" She straightened, leaning forward, eyes wide. "Why those two could have been twins, they looked that alike. Claire - that was the nurse's name, poor dear. She was a bit taller, and Jenny had that terrible limp. She often had to walk with a cane, it was so bad."

"How about their voices?" Marissa asked. "Did they sound alike?"

"Why no, not at all. Claire had a bit of a southern drawl, a Texas twang I think she called it." She frowned, staring at Marissa for a moment. "What on earth would that have to do with finding Jenny?"

"Maybe everything, Sarah," Marissa answered, leaning forward. "I'm going to ask you a strange question and I want you to try your best to remember the last time Jenny came in, just before she left Timberville." The woman nodded, still frowning. "Are you absolutely certain the woman at your house that day was Jenny Benedict?"

Sarah Hanes leaned back in her seat. Her right hand closed into a loose fist rising to her chin until her thumb rested just below her lower lip. She tapped her thumb on her lip occasionally, as if punctuating a thought. Finally, she straightened. "Why you know, I'm not sure. She had that limp, and her voice, well it was lower in pitch. She mentioned suffering some vocal cord damage from the explosion when I asked her if she was okay…" her voice trailed off.

"Miss Maines mentioned a phone call Jennifer made from here," Marissa continued. Sarah nodded.

"Do you remember any details about the call, anything at all?"

"I remember she called Claire's sister. The sister hadn't been told about Claire until after they buried what was left of her, poor dear. Oh she was fit to be tied, I tell you! I could hear her yelling all the way from the kitchen." She shook her head. "Funny now I think about it, how quick Jenny calmed her down I mean. It wasn't more than a minute."

"What did Jenny say to her?"

"Why I don't know. She talked low and I couldn't make it out from the kitchen." She poured more tea for herself and the librarian. Marissa hadn't touched hers. "I wasn't eavesdropping you know," she added, testily. "The sister was yelling so loud I couldn't help knowing how angry she was." She tapped a finger on the teacup she held. "It was so long ago."

Marissa thanked her and left the two women reminiscing about the year of the fire. She stopped at the motel office to check for messages, finding a note in the room slot with Harvey's standard "Call home" scribbled on it. In her room, she dialed his office.

"What've you got for me, Harve?"

"Nothing special. Mildred Kryzynski is a retired teacher, lives in Lubbock, no husband or kids." She heard him shuffling papers. "We haven't got bank account info yet. I'll let you know soon as we do."

Marissa took a deep breath. "Time to visit Jenny," she said.

"I'll send backup."

"I think it's better if I see her alone."

"You sure?"

"I'll head out first thing in the morning."

Chapter 28

Two hours after sunrise the following day Marissa bounced up the rutted path past Jethro's place and eased the van into Jenny's packed dirt yard. As she stepped out of the van, Jenny appeared from the barn, a twelve-gauge pump shotgun tucked in the crook of her arm. Marissa stopped, partly shielded by the open door, her right hand touching the Glok-40 clamped to the door panel.

"We need to talk," Marissa said.

"About what?"

"We'd be a lot more comfortable if you'd put down the shotgun."

"You, maybe. Not me." Jenny pumped a round into the chamber but didn't raise the weapon. "Why are you here? I told you you couldn't have Milo. I meant it."

"It's not about him, but we still need to talk." Marissa had the Glok in her hand now, still hidden from Jenny's view. She saw a flicker of motion in the trees then Milo silently rounded the corner of the barn out of Jenny's view and froze, eyes wide. "I said it's not about Milo ..." she flicked the safety off. "... but you and I have some things to clear up."

Jenny stepped closer, grip tightening on the shotgun. Milo edged along the side of the barn, closing the distance between him and his two mothers; confusion and fear contorted his features. Marissa wished he'd not shown up. "Get back in your car and get out!" Jenny ordered.

Eyes on Jenny's hands, Marissa balanced on the balls of her feet. "I can't do that ... Claire."

What happened next, happened quickly. Jenny's eyes went wide. She raised the shotgun. Marissa dove to her left when Jenny fired, discharging two rounds at her from the Glok as she did. Several pellets tore at Marissa's leg and torso on her way to the ground. She rolled, hitting her head on a corner of the tool shed, heard another loud blast, and saw Jenny fall before she blacked out. When she regained consciousness, JT was kneeling over her, cutting away the leg of her jeans.

"JT?"

"Keep still. Looks like nothing vital got hit." He gently lifted the side of her shirt. "It'll take some work to dig the birdshot out but you're pretty lucky."

Wincing, Marissa pushed into a sitting position against the tool shed wall. "Jenny?"

"Pretty bad." Seeing the question in Marissa's eyes, JT shook his head. "Wasn't me. The old shotgun blew up in her face when she tried to pump another round into you. Best I can figure, they were old shells, and part of the first one never left the chamber. Which, by the way, is probably the reason you're alive. When she jacked in another round and squeezed the trigger the old gun came apart; lodged part of itself in her skull from the look."

Marissa nodded. Looking past JT with a worried frown she asked, "Milo?"

"The boy? Disappeared like a shadow on a cloudy day." He rose and nodded in Jenny's direction. "I'm going to do what I can to stabilize her. Then I'll get you two down the mountain."

Marissa rose and limped toward the barn. Near the point where she'd seen Milo, there were drops of blood. Scared now, she rounded the corner but saw only the barely visible track Milo made on his way into the woods. "I've got to find him."

"Doesn't look bad," JT said from just behind her. "Not a whole lot of blood. Looks venous. I saw him spin and fall when the shooting started. I'm guessing one of your rounds ricocheted and hit him." He returned to the center of the yard and knelt at Jenny's side.

"You need to get those BB's plucked," he called. "I'll send someone back for the boy as soon as I get you two to civilization."

"Nobody else will be able to find him, JT. I've got to go." Marissa took a breath then limped to her van. She slid open the side door and hoisted herself in then faced him. "It would be a real help if you could get a medical team up here in the next few hours." Turning away, she opened a long cabinet and extracted a jumpsuit. She pulled off her jeans and shirt, tossing them into the corner then opened the drawer with her first aid kit and went to work on her wounds.

"Sure you won't come down with us?" He called from the yard.

"I'll be fine. Just get a med team here." She winced as she applied the antiseptic. "How's she look?"

"Vitals are okay for now. I want to keep that chunk of steel in her skull from moving around but I'm afraid to get near it." He stood and faced Marissa. "Any ideas?"

She shook her head then she noticed the mule grazing on the far side of a small field. "What about a horse collar?"

"Might work," JT said and hurried toward the open barn door. Half a minute later, he returned with an armload of harness pieces and a board about six-feet long. Soon he had Jenny lying on the board with her head and neck anchored. Satisfied he stood, turned, and double-timed down the old road.

Marissa watched until he disappeared around the corner then completed her repairs and dressed. She was locking the van when JT's SUV rounded the corner.

Together they got Jenny into the back. They secured her in place with straps both to stop her from shifting on the trip out, and to keep her under control in the event she regained consciousness. Marissa turned away and hurried toward the woods before JT started the vehicle.

"Good luck!" he yelled. She waved without looking back and disappeared around the corner of the barn.

JT was right about the blood, it was sparse and dark; a good sign. Her only concern now was to get to Milo before he attempted to dig the bullet out and caused unnecessary damage. She was pretty sure he'd wait until he got to his cave before thinking about what to do next. She'd seen him bounce thoughts and alternatives around in his mind, picking out the best with careful precision, giving a single nod when the solution surfaced. "I hope he thinks long and hard before trying to remove that bullet," she mumbled, picking up her pace in spite of the pain.

Marissa missed Milo's change in direction at first, realizing her error only when she hadn't seen sign of his passing for more than a hundred feet. She backtracked and picked up his trail heading toward Jethro's place. Another half mile and he shifted direction again, angling back toward the mountaintop. Marissa picked up her pace, concerned that the changes might mean he was hurt worse than she'd thought. A short time later he turned yet again, making for the cabin.

His move had been too visible to be an attempt to throw off anyone following; no, he was confused and hurt, and a teenage boy. He was going home to mama. *He doesn't know*, Marissa thought. She broke into a run, oblivious of the pain shooting through her right side. When she rounded the barn, she saw Milo kneeling, head down in the middle of the clearing where Jenny's blood had clumped the dust as it seeped into the brown earth. The shattered shotgun rested across his lap. He didn't raise his head, though she was certain he heard her approach.

"Milo?" She circled him, out of his reach, until they were facing each other across the dampness. Grimacing, she squatted on her haunches then she rolled to her knees. "Milo?"

He looked at her; tears streaked his dusty cheeks. They knelt that way for several long seconds until he finally spoke. "Maw daid?"

"I don't know, Milo." Marissa's eyes went to his left arm, to the dark stain and the trickle of blood rolling down his triceps. "I want to see your arm, okay?"

"It ain't nothin'."

"Let me look … please?" He shook his head.

It seemed he was about to get up when his eyes widened, his head cocked to the side and he pointed to her leg. "Y'all bleedin'. Wus that Maw?"

Marissa looked down at the widening stain and nodded. "Please let me look at your arm?" She rose too quickly and stumbled forward into Milo, taking them both to the ground. He yelped as his shoulder hit the packed earth. "I'm sorry, Milo," she said, struggling to push herself into a kneeling position.

Milo lay where he'd fallen, his breath coming in short gasps. Marissa pulled Milo's knife from the sheath on his belt and cut the sleeve of his T-shirt all the way to the neck. Dropping the knife in the dirt, she peeled back the fabric revealing a jagged entry wound at the top of his bicep. She gritted her teeth and, very gently turned him away from her. No exit wound. She rolled him back. He was wide-eyed, terrified. She checked her watch. Eleven-twenty. *Keep him still,* was her mantra as she checked to see if there were any more wounds.

"Milo? Can you hear me?"

He mouthed "Yes."

"Good." She tried to relax her face, tried to remove the fear from her eyes, before she continued. "Good. I'm going to run over to my van and get something to keep you warm. Now this is important Milo. I want you to stay completely still; don't move a muscle. Do you understand?"

Another mouthed "yes."

Marissa hurried to the van, cursing as she fumbled for her keys. She slid the side door wide with a bang. Gathering blankets, water, her first aid kit, and her portable two-way radio, she hurried back to Milo. His eyes were closed; sweat beaded on his brow, and his breathing was ragged.

Marissa knelt beside him. "Stay with me, Milo. You hear?" She said as she covered him with the blankets. She started to give him water then thought that if he coughed the bullet inside him might shift again, so she soaked a bandana and pressed it gently to his lips. He suckled it like a baby, her baby.

Terror was a feeling she hadn't experienced since … since she lived up here with the animal that fathered Milo. She had to do something or she'd scream. *Talk, Missy, just say words, any words.* She bit her lip, soaked the bandana with a fresh supply of water and leaned close to him.

"Milo, the bullet that hit you … it hit something else first." His eyelids fluttered. "I know because it was wobbling when it got to you, your wound … the hole in your shoulder, told me that." Marissa hesitated, wondering if he needed to hear the rest, then continued because *she* had to hear it. "Because it hit something else, it was slowed down so it didn't go all the way through and out the other side. It … it bounced off one of your bones and

209

went into your body somewhere. Right now it's what's making it hard for you to breathe."

Milo opened his mouth. She thought he wanted to speak but his eyes told her he wanted the bandana. She doused it again and pressed it to his lips.

"My friend has taken your maw to the hospital and he'll be back very soon with some people who will help you." *Make it very, very soon, JT.* "We're just going to be very still until they get here." When her own breath started coming in ragged bursts, Marissa realized she was crying.

Chapter 29

It took several seconds for Marissa to identify the approaching sound as the rotors of a helicopter. She watched it come to rest in the small pasture, stampeding the mule to the farthest corner of the field. JT hopped out before the rotors stopped and hurried toward her, followed by two medics. When they got closer, he stepped aside pointing to the boy on the ground.

"The bullet's somewhere inside him," Marissa said. "It wobbled … didn't go through. It … it's in him. I stumbled and … "

"We've got it ma'am," the taller one said, kneeling. He glanced at Marissa's right leg and nodded to the other medic. "Jim …"

Jim crouched next to her. "Let me take a look at that."

"No, it's alright." She pushed him away. "You've got to …"

"C'mon, Marissa," JT said, touching her shoulder. "Let them work." He held out his hand. Marissa took it, using it to help her stand. She winced as she straightened her injured right leg. The shorter medic, Jim, spoke into his radio and seconds later another figure emerged from the side door of the helicopter, carrying a backboard and a blaze orange canvas bag.

It took several minutes for the medics to position Milo on the board and restrict his movement with pads and straps. They carried him to the helicopter, Marissa and JT following closely behind.

She turned to JT when they reached the door. "I'm going with him." He nodded and helped her into the machine just as the engine coughed to life and the rotors began spinning.

"I'll bring your van," he yelled over the din.

She patted her pockets then remembered. "They're in the door."

On the ride to the heliport on top of University Hospital in Harrisonburg, Marissa watched the two medics work to keep her son alive, talking into the headsets they'd donned. One part of her wished she could hear them, another wasn't sure she wanted to. She refused again to let Jim check her wound, wanting his attention focused on Milo.

Three women waited with a gurney in front of an open door near the edge of the pad. As soon as the machine settled onto the surface they hurried toward it, crouching under the still spinning blades. The medics and two of the women, Marissa assumed they were nurses, moved Milo onto the gurney. The third woman touched a stethoscope to Milo's chest in several places then said something that Marissa couldn't hear, and they all hurried toward a waiting elevator. Marissa hopped out of the door to follow but her right leg folded under her and she fell sideways. Jim was immediately at her side.

"Stay right there, ma'am. I'll get another gurney." She grabbed his arm as he started to rise.

"Help me up," she said. "I can walk."

"You sure?"

"Just give me a shoulder to lean on."

"If I do, I want you in that wheelchair over by the door as soon as we reach it, deal?" She nodded.

When the elevator door opened, Jim wheeled Marissa into the hall where another nurse waited. "Thanks, Jimmy. I'll take it from here." He turned her chair over to the nurse and stepped back into the elevator just as the doors closed.

"I need to see my son."

"He's in the OR right now. He's in good hands. Let's go take care of you."

"Look, I'm FBI." She put her hands on the arms of the chair. "My son's in there and I'm going to see him."

The nurse put her hands on Marissa's shoulders. "I'm Corrine, Miss FBI, and you couldn't get into Dr. Klein's OR if you were God." Corrine pushed the chair into a room on the right. "Now, can you get onto the table by yourself or do you need some help?"

Suddenly Marissa felt incredibly tired. Wincing she pushed herself to her feet and hobbled to the table. She let nurse Corrine help her up then lay back on the cool sheet.

"Sit up for a minute, Miss FBI."

"Marissa."

"Okay, Marissa, sit up." She obeyed. "Let's get this jumpsuit off so we can see where you're hurting." Soon Marissa was lying on the table under a light cotton blanket, naked except for a hospital gown. The nurse left, returning a few minutes later with a cart containing a basin of water and several folded towels. "Okay, let's get you cleaned up." She lifted the blanket off Marissa's right side. "Still a little blood oozing from one of them," nurse Corrine said.

"How's my son?"

"Still in the OR. Roll on your left side for me." The nurse washed the dried blood from Marissa's leg then examined her wounds. "The shotgun blast carved a couple of grooves in your side, and one went completely through, just under the skin. You also have four pellets lodged in your quadriceps. One's pretty deep, but I can actually see the others." She pressed a gauze pad on Marissa's leg, causing her to wince. "Sorry. Dr. Klein will get those out just as soon as she's finished with your son. Lie back now." She dressed the wounds in Marissa's side, covered her with the blanket then left with the cart.

Chapter 30

"Miss Landry? Marissa? "

Marissa opened her eyes. She recognized the woman standing by her side as the doctor who'd met the helicopter. "Doctor Klein?"

The woman looked up from the clipboard. "Yes."

"How is my son?"

Dr. Klein removed her reading glasses, letting them hang from the cord around her neck. "That boy is your son?" She frowned at the nurse. "I'm sorry I didn't know that."

"How is he?"

"He's in recovery right now. He'll be fine." She handed Marissa's chart to the nurse. "Before we put him under, he asked about you. He wanted to know if you were dead."

"What did you tell him?"

"I didn't tell him anything. We put him out pretty quickly." She lifted Marissa's blanket. "Let's take a look." Marissa rolled onto her left side. The doctor removed the dressing and examined each wound. When she finished she turned to the nurse. "I want an x-ray then prep her and bring her to my OR." She faced Marissa. "I need to see exactly where the pellets are, especially the deepest one, before we take them out." She patted Marissa's arm then turned to leave.

"I want to see my son."

Dr Klein turned back. "He's still asleep. Let's get those pellets taken care of then you can see him. We'll need to get some more information from you also, but it can wait."

215

Milo's Gift

Weary, Marissa closed her eyes and let herself be wheeled out of the room.

Chapter 31

"How're you feeling, Marissa?"

She heard the voice as if from the far end of a long tunnel. The shadowy form at the foot of her bed morphed into JT as her vision cleared. "Sleepy."

"Harvey's flying up from Richmond. He should be here in about an hour."

"Why?"

"He wants to make sure you're okay." She nodded, eyes closing.

She shook her head, trying to clear it. "Milo?"

"Just across the hall. He's pretty groggy. The nurse says it's from the pain medication."

Marissa tried to sit up. "I want to see him." A wave of nausea forced her back down.

"Doesn't look like you're going anywhere just yet."

She took a couple of deep breaths. "JT, he's just been through hell and he's alone in a hospital." She tried sitting up again and failed. "He needs a friendly face."

JT nodded. "Let me see what I can do." He squeezed her toes through the blanket. "Be right back."

Marissa watched him leave, thought about trying to rise again, rejecting the thought. Instead she lifted the cover to look at her right leg. All she could see was the dressing that covered the wounds. She dropped the blanket, aware now of the dull ache radiating from the area.

JT returned a few minutes later, nurse Corrine in tow. "Agent Marshall tells me you'd like to see your son." Marissa nodded. "We're going to wheel you into the room with him." She checked Marissa's IV then pushed a foot pedal on the bed and moved it so the headboard was angled toward the door. JT grabbed the foot of the bed and helped navigate it across the wide hallway. They positioned it in the empty area next to Milo, close enough for Marissa to reach out and touch the boy. "How's that?" the nurse asked.

Marissa smiled. "Thanks, Corrine." The nurse patted her arm, did a quick check of the various wires and tubes attached to Milo then left.

JT tapped the foot of the bed. "I'm going to the airport to get the boss." He squeezed her toes again.

"Thanks JT," she called to his back. He raised a hand without turning and disappeared through the door.

She watched Milo's chest rise and fall, comforted by the regularity of his breathing.

****

Marissa was dozing when Dr. Klein entered the room. She watched the doctor lift the sheet covering Milo's left side, watched her stare at the monitor, watched her open one of the two charts she held and write something in it. "How is he?" Marissa finally asked.

Klein looked up, smiling. "He's progressing quite well." She left Milo's side and walked around the foot of both beds until she stood next to Marissa. She closed Milo's chart and opened the other one, placing both on the rolling table next to Marissa's bed. "Let's have a look." Folding the sheet away from Marissa's right leg, the doctor examined the four tiny wounds. "I didn't need to stitch them, but I took a stitch in each anyway; less scarring. The deep one was a fraction of an inch from the femoral artery. You got lucky." She covered Marissa's leg, wrote on her chart then said, "Agent Marshall told me this was all the result of a gun battle when you tried to arrest someone. I'm going to need some details to file my report with the police." The doctor folded back the first sheet of

Marissa's chart then rested her elbows on the table. "What happened out there? And what was your son doing in the middle of it?"

Just as Marissa was about to respond, Nurse Corrine burst through the door. "Doctor Klein, there's an obnoxious old man in a wheelchair out in the hall saying he's Miss Landry's boss and demanding to see her. I told him you were examining her, but he ..."

"Out of my way!" Harvey Delancey yelled, rolling through the open door.

"Stop right there!" Dr. Klein ordered. Delancey stopped.

"I'm here to see Agent Landry," he demanded.

"So I heard." The doctor stepped toward him, hands on her hips. "You may be some FBI big shot, but you're in my hospital now, and you're going to apologize to my nurse then roll your ass back through that door until I call you."

Face turning the color of raw steak, Delancey sputtered, "Why I ..."

"It's okay, Harv," Marissa interrupted, laughing. "Dr. Klein was just asking me what happened on the mountain. If you apologize to Nurse Corrine, and mean it, she might let you stay."

Delancey growled, spun his chair toward the door where the nurse cowered, then spun back to glare at Marissa. He released a deep sigh then, smiling his sweetest smile turned back toward the nurse. "I'm sorry."

"Is that an acceptable apology, Corrine?" Marissa asked. The nurse nodded, grinning. "Doctor, do you mind if this grumpy old man stays?"

"Maw! Where's Maw?" Milo, eyes wide, tried to sit but collapsed coughing.

Dr. Klein was at his side immediately. "Easy Milo, your mother is right here."

Marissa focused on Delancey. "Harve, what about Jenny?"

"Evac'd to Shock Trauma at UM Medical." He shrugged. "Last I knew she was in surgery. That was …" he glanced at his watch, "a little over four hours ago."

"Can you get an update?" she asked.

He spun his chair around. "Nurse, I need an outside line." Corrine hurried through the door, motioning for him to follow.

When they were gone, Marissa swung her legs over the side of the bed, wincing when her right leg flexed at the knee. JT grabbed her shoulders from behind, steadying her. She took a breath then nodded without turning and he released his hold. "Dr Klein, may I speak with Milo alone?"

The doctor glanced at Marissa over her shoulder then stepped away and strode toward the door, stopping at the jamb. "I'll be right down the hall. Try to keep him calm."

"JT?"

"I'm gone." He followed the doctor through the door.

Marissa turned toward Milo's bed. His eyes, wide and frightened, were scanning the room. "Milo? It's Marissa. Look at me, please." When he turned toward her voice, she could see tension in the muscles of his jaw. "I've sent someone to find out about your maw." She placed her hand on his arm. "She was hurt pretty badly when the shotgun blew up."

Milo's eyes swung left and right; he blinked, frowned then stared directly at Marissa. "Maw.. she wus gonna kill ya, wadn't she?" Marissa nodded. He lay back, looking at the ceiling so intently that she thought he might be counting holes in the acoustic tiles. It was a long minute before he spoke again. "She kilt paw."

Marissa straightened. "You saw her?"

"Din't 'member til just now." His frown deepened. "I wus … it wus long time ago. Mebbe eight – ten year."

"Can you tell me about it?"

Milo closed his eyes. Marissa waited, and waited. "Milo?" No response. "Milo? Talk to me. Please?"

He blinked twice. "Hard."

"I'm sure it is." She hesitated hoping he'd continue. When he didn't, she prodded, "Was he … was Paw, hurting your maw?"

More silence, then, "Uh huh." His hands opened and closed several times before he continued. "They wus blood … her face … Paw wus drunk. He hit Maw … knocked 'er down." Milo breathed rapidly. "Paw tried to … to kick 'er. He tripped, 'n Maw … she jumped on 'im, took his skinnin' knife out his belt, 'n stuck his neck." He bit his lip, eyes tearing. "She kep' stickin' 'n twistin' the knife. Paw howled for a time, tryin' t' throw Maw … couldn't shake 'er. Pretty soon he din't move no more." His tears flowed freely. "Maw kep' stickin' 'n twistin'."

Marissa touched his arm. "That's enough, Milo. Enough." She stood beside him, stroking his hair. "Easy, honey, easy."

Marissa stayed beside Milo until he quieted and finally slept. Wincing, she crawled into her own bed and pushed the button that raised the head end until she felt comfortable. She tried to get her head around Milo's description. Remembering how Larson had tossed her into the brush easily as he would have an empty beer bottle, she was awed by what Jenny had been able to do. At the sound of a wheelchair in the hall, she turned her attention toward the door. When Delancey came through, she put a finger to her lips. Nodding, he rolled to the side of her bed farthest from Milo and stopped.

"Jenny?"

Delancey shook his head. "She didn't make it. Died on the table."

Marissa sighed. "I'll tell him."

"You sure?" She nodded. "Have you thought about what's next for the two of you?"

Startled, she was about to ask Delancey what he meant when she realized that Milo, her son Milo, was unquestionably her responsibility. "I don't know."

"You have some down time coming, what with rehab and vacation."

"It won't take me long to get back."

"It will take as long as I say it takes." She glared at him. "Don't give me that look. In spite of your continuing insubordination, I'm still your boss." He backed the chair up out of her immediate reach. "Your van, which I believe contains every FBI authorized weapon that is not one of your body parts, is in the parking garage and I have the keys. I issued you a sedan for the duration of your rehab." He spun around and headed for the door. "You have a two-bedroom waiting in Quantico when you leave here."

"Harve?"

He stopped and turned. "Yeah?"

"Thanks," she said. He grunted and rolled through the door.

Delancey's question mushroomed into a bunch of her own. How could she bring Milo into civilization? What should happen with the mountain property? What about his education? Jesus, what about getting shoes on him even? She'd given birth to this boy but was not his mother in any real sense. His mother was dead.

Yet more questions swirled in her head as she dozed, until exhaustion overtook her.

Chapter 32

"Marissa? M … Missy?" Milo's voice broke into Marissa's dream, pulling her awake.

She turned toward his bed, propping herself on her elbow. "Right here, Milo." His head was turned so that he could see her. "How are you feeling?" she asked. He nodded. She watched his face, intrigued by how readily its expressions revealed his thought process. She waited for the question, stealing herself for the answer.

"Maw daid?"

"Yes." He blinked back tears, nodded, blinked some more and finally let go a howling sob that brought the duty nurse into the room. Marissa explained the situation.

"He should be kept quiet," she scolded. "He's recovering from a gunshot wound."

Irritated by the nurse's tone, Marissa responded, "I know. I shot him." She regretted the statement as soon as she said it. Milo choked back his sobs and stared at her, his features contorted.

The horrified nurse stood open-mouthed. "Look, I'm the boy's mother." That didn't seem to ease the nurse's mind at all so Marissa focused all her attention on Milo. "Milo, listen. Let me explain." She searched for words that would get past the horror in his eyes. Finally, she swung her legs over the side of the bed ignoring the pain, stood and forced the nurse out the door, closing it after her. Marissa hurried to Milo's bed and sat beside him. He slid away from her, too weak to do much else.

Marissa took a long breath. "When your maw shot at me, I dove sideways to avoid getting killed. While I was moving, I fired my weapon." She shook her head. "You might not remember this, but I told you the bullet that hit

you had hit something else first. Do you remember?"
Milo's eyes flicked back and forth for a moment then he
nodded. "One of my shots must have glanced off the
barrel of the shotgun and hit you." She put both hands on
his shoulders feeling him tense. "You have to believe me,
Milo. I would never shoot at you ... never. You're my
son." Marissa searched his face, hoping.

Finally, putting a period on his thought process
with that telltale little nod, he responded. "Maw tried t' kill
ya?" Marissa nodded. He rested his head on the pillow
and closed his eyes.

The sadness Marissa had seen in those eyes
wrenched at her heart. "It will be alright," she whispered.
"I promise."

She stood and turned as the door opened. Finger
to her lips, she approached the nurse and the security
guard. "He's sleeping. Let's go into the hall so I can
explain."

Chapter 33

Four days later Marissa was pacing the living room of her new apartment, trying to prioritize the many tasks created by Milo's presence in her life. She'd ridden with him in the ambulance from Harrisonburg to the Army hospital at Fort Belvoir. Dr. Klein had refused to release him until Marissa assured her Milo would remain hospitalized for at least another week. In many ways Marissa was thankful for the time.

Reports from the hospital told her Milo was up and moving around, amusing and sometimes annoying the staff with endless questions about the equipment he saw. In the three days he'd been at the hospital, he'd apparently learned to use a blood pressure cuff by convincing the nurses to let him try it on them after they'd taken his pressure. He'd walk through the halls peeking into open rooms, sometimes walking in to visit with the occupants, until the staff convinced him that he could spread infection from one room to the next. Those trips introduced him to the machines that monitored heartbeats and other vital signs. He asked questions about the spikes and numbers he saw on the screen and soon was able to identify irregularities as quickly as the nurses he followed. These reports both impressed and in many ways scared her. He learned so quickly that she wondered how she'd be able to keep him motivated.

More troubling was his coldness toward her when she visited. He responded to her questions but didn't engage in conversation. He flinched when she touched him. She left each visit feeling sad and angry.

Desperate, she called Delancey. "Harve, I can't reach him. He hates me."

"You have to give him time to deal with the new information, Missy Mae."

"But it's been almost a week."

Delancey's short laugh startled her. "Look girl, that might be a long time if you'd blurted out that he had a wart on his nose, but when you tell the boy his new-found mom put a bullet in him, that's likely to take a little longer to process."

She sat on the sofa. Swinging her legs onto the cushions, she massaged the newly healed wounds. "How long?"

"Missy, I'm a shrink, not a shaman. As long as it takes." His tone softened. "Remember this, though. You are his mother and he knows that."

"Will you come visit him?"

"No, I'm too close to you. Hang on." He put her on hold before she could answer. Five minutes later she heard, "Still there?"

"Yeah?"

"I contacted a psychiatrist I know at Belvoir."

She sighed, "Is he good?"

"Yeah, almost as good as me."

"I want to meet him," she said, "And it's 'I'."

He laughed. "You're a pain in the ass. I'll set it up for this afternoon. You're still on leave, so leave." He hung up.

Marissa called the gym, arranged a session with the martial arts instructor and spent an hour sparring. Relaxed and a little bruised, she showered and dressed. On her way back to the apartment, she decided two things: she would not push Milo to forgive her, and she would stop apologizing for the bullet.

Two hours later she stepped off the elevator onto the third floor of the hospital's pediatric wing and almost ran into Milo, who was talking with a pretty young medic. "Oops! Hi Milo," she said, forcing a smile. "Who's your friend?"

The medic stepped forward, extending her hand. "Spec-five Jessica Stone, ma'am." Milo, head down, took a step back. "Milo and I were just heading for physical therapy."

"Marissa Landry, FBI." She shook the young woman's hand. "Glad to meet you." Aware of Milo's small movements, she fought the temptation to address him directly, focusing instead on Jessica Stone – reading her eyes, her body language, her attraction to Milo.

"She's m' maw," Milo offered, quietly. The medic nodded without turning toward him.

"You've become quite a legend around here, ma'am."

Marissa frowned. "How so?"

The medic reached for Milo's arm, pulling him close. "Milo here talks about you all the time." His cheeks reddened, his face crinkling in a funny grin. "According to him you could track a beetle over rocks." Milo's face turned crimson.

Marissa laughed. "Well, if it was a big beetle with wet feet, maybe." She reached for Milo's hand. With only slight hesitation, he gave it to her. "We've been through a whole lot of hard stuff recently." She squeezed his hand and felt the return pressure. "But, I think things are going to get better soon."

-END-

www.ingramcontent.com/pod-product-compliance
Lightning Source LLC
Chambersburg PA
CBHW030539030726
47495CB00004B/1055